The Victory Snapshot

Also by Barrie Roberts:

Sherlock Holmes and the Railway Maniac
Sherlock Holmes and the Devil's Grail
Sherlock Holmes and the Man From Hell

THE VICTORY SNAPSHOT

Barrie Roberts

Constable · London

First published in Great Britain 1997
by Constable & Company Ltd
3 The Lanchesters
162 Fulham Palace Road
London W6 9ER
Copyright © 1997 Barrie Roberts
The right of Barrie Roberts to be
identified as the author of this work
has been asserted by him in accordance
with the Copyright, Designs and Patents Act 1988
ISBN 0 09 477670 9
Set in Palatino 10 pt by
SetSystems Ltd, Saffron Walden, Essex
Printed and bound in Great Britain by
MPG Books Ltd, Bodmin, Cornwall

A CIP catalogue record for this book
is available from the British Library

Note

The Metropolitan Borough of Belston does not exist. If it did, it would probably be one of the so-called 'Black Country Boroughs' that lie north-west of Birmingham; since it doesn't, it isn't. All characters and events in this story are completely fictitious, with one exception.

The one exception is the crime around which this story revolves. It did take place, though not in the Midlands. As in the story, the criminals were never sought, arrested nor punished, which raises interesting speculations as to who they were and what became of them.

Barrie Roberts
1997

1

'Cadaveric spasm', declaimed Dr Macintyre, giving all six syllables a resonant Scots roll over his tongue, 'is the pathological phenomenon least understood by the writers of cheap detective novels, to whom it serves as a gruesome device in their ill-thought-out plots. It is, in fact, never found in cases of stabbing and rarely in gunshot or head wound cases. Nevertheless, it is present in this instance.'

He paused, and gazed down at the long, pale corpse on the steel mortuary table before continuing. 'Deceased's right hand was tightly clenched. Examination revealed . . .'

This time he stopped to look around him. The only witness to his lecture was a pallid detective constable, standing as far away from the table as possible and trying not to listen to Macintyre's oration. The constable was longing for fresh air and a cigarette; only the voice-operated cassette recorder was paying attention.

Macintyre picked up a steel implement from a trolley and applied it to the cadaver's clenched fist, prying the bony fingers open, one by one. Something dropped from the hand and rang on the satin steel examination table. Picking it up, the doctor straightened and drew a deep, noisy breath. The reels of the recorder stirred silently as he continued, '. . . a small object firmly held . . .'

No, I wasn't there on that particular occasion, but I've had the rare privilege of watching Dr Macintyre at work, and that will be the way it happened. Doc's province, the Borough Mortuary, is discreetly tucked away up an alley alongside the Guildhall. It doesn't have a sign on it. The customers don't have to find their own way; they all get chauffeur-driven.

While Doc was making his discovery I was in a better-known

part of the building – the magistrates' court. The Crown Prosecutor was on his feet, cross-examining a lanky, blue-eyed Irishman who kept irritating the magistrates by trying to put his hat on in the witness box.

'Now, Mr Murphy, when did you come to Belston?'

The Irishman looked confused. 'I can't just recall', he said, 'if that was before Christmas or after Christmas.'

The tubby, silver-haired Prosecutor rolled an unbelieving eye at the Bench. 'You don't know where you spent Christmas?' he asked, wonderingly.

'Oh, yes, sir. I was in Manchester for Christmas. I remember that, sir.'

The Prosecutor smiled. 'That's better,' he said. 'So you came here after Christmas?'

It wasn't better. Murphy shook his head. 'Oh no, sir. I wasn't saying that. You see, I always spend Christmas in Manchester, wherever I've been. If I was here before Christmas I'd have gone down to Manchester for Christmas and if I was somewheres else before I'd have gone to Manchester for Christmas and then come here after.'

'Come now, Mr Murphy,' said the Prosecutor, 'you can do better than that. What religion are you?'

'I'm a Roman Catholic, sir,' replied Murphy, stoutly.

'Good,' said the Prosecutor. 'So you know when Christmas is?'

'I know it's 25th December, sir, but I don't know what day that was. I think it was Wednesday this year.'

Along the lawyers' table from the Prosecutor, at the defence end, I was leaning over my papers and trying to stifle snorts of amusement. Christmas Day had been a Monday, and I suspect that my client well knew it.

Entangled in Murphy's logic, the Prosecutor retreated and attacked from another direction.

'You brought a caravan and a lorry from Manchester last winter,' he said. 'Are you trying to tell the court that you can't remember even roughly when that was?'

'But I didn't,' protested Murphy.

'You didn't what?' asked the lawyer.

8

'I didn't bring a trailer and a lorry. I had two trailers and me big lorry and a transit van.'

'Right,' said the Prosecutor. 'So you brought four vehicles here. You must remember when that was.'

'No, sir,' said the Irishman. 'You see, me wife would have driven the lorry and me oldest boy had the transit. I came up by the train, but I don't know when that was.' He paused. 'It was snowing when I came,' he added helpfully.

I couldn't help it; I snorted again, audibly, and earned a reproving frown from the chairman.

Eventually even the Prosecutor saw that he was getting nowhere. After brief closing speeches, the clerk had a whispered word with the chairman of the Bench. He said, 'Wouldn't you like to adjourn to the back room for a cup of tea?', and the magistrates, whose verdict of guilty had been legible on their faces since before the defence opened, agreed with alacrity.

The clerk rose and shuffled his papers. 'Their Worships are retiring to consider their decision,' he announced. 'All rise!'

The Prosecutor and I stood up, the idlers in the public gallery slouched to their feet, a bored pressman half stood and the usher at the back woke and rushed to the door that led into the retiring room, whipping it open just as the three magistrates reached it.

Behind me I could hear legs being stretched in the public seats. I sat and played Hangman with myself on my scrap pad while I imagined Their Worships' deliberations.

In the panelled room behind the court they would have poured themselves tea and be standing around chatting, stretching their own legs. Major Billingham, who had been impatient ever since Murphy pleaded 'Not guilty', would be looking at his watch. Billingham was new to our Bench and had been glancing at his watch throughout the defence case. Now he would be telling the chairman that he'd heard my cases were long drawn-out jobs, but half a day for an obstruction by a tinker was going it a bit strong.

The chairman would chuckle and warn him that he'd have to get used to me. He would explain that every town has its 'layabouts' lawyer' and I was Belston's. 'Came here about ten years ago as assistant to old Humphreys,' he would say. 'Lasted about six months before they had some kind of row, then he set up on his own. Started out with one room, one desk, two chairs – that sort of practice. Makes his living defending tinkers, hippies, drug addicts, Pakis, blacks, all the anti-social elements – even racist hooligans.'

He would finish sipping his tea and tell his colleagues, 'Let's get back in there and pot his bloody client. That'll teach him to waste our time.'

They were still chortling at this pleasantry when they filed back into court and their clerk brayed, 'Be upstanding for Their Worships.'

My name is Tyroll, Christopher Tyroll, Solicitor of the Supreme Court. Thirty-five years old, single (not my choice – my ex-wife's), religion vaguely Christian, politics vaguely leftish. Smoker, moderate drinker. Medium height, slim and darkly good-looking according to my mirror, 'slight and skinny and looks like some kind of foreigner' if you believe my professional colleagues. Sole support of an assistant solicitor, an articled clerk, a secretary, a typist and an office junior, all corporately known as 'Tyrolls' – an overburdened legal aid practice which threatens to go into liquidation about thirty times a month, even in February.

Paddy Murphy was philosophical about his conviction and polite about my unsuccessful efforts. Outside the court he scratched his balding head, jammed his battered old tweed hat firmly in place, shook my hand warmly and sauntered off in search of a drink. I would have joined him, but you can't interview clients with your breath smelling of booze, so I hefted my briefcase and headed for the Rendezvous.

The Rendezvous Café has stood in the shadow of the Guild-hall as long as anyone can remember. It was born in the twenties and it shows. Almost every year someone tries to get it pulled down, on the perfectly truthful basis that its peeling frontage and enamelled signs offering forgotten brands of cigarettes and soft drinks are an eyesore and a blot on the square, but it survives.

Its longevity is due to powerful friends. Most of the lawyers in Belston have known the Rendezvous since their childhood, and come to love it when they were articled clerks. It's the last port of call for a hurried cuppa before court in the morning, a place to meet clients and witnesses, and a place to have a leisurely afternoon cup with toasted teacakes before returning to the office. In their later careers, as local politicians, none of its denizens have ever been able to order its demolition.

For half an hour in the morning it's a maelstrom as lawyers, policemen and half the town's petty villains press at the counters for mugs of tea. Later the victims return, cursing at their fines, and on market days you'll find it full until the last stalls close, but today it was empty.

Two overalled ladies, one maternally plump and one neurotically thin, lolled at the counter discussing last night's *East-Enders*. In a cubicle at the rear, where the afternoon sun did not penetrate, their sole customer hunched over a mug of orange-coloured tea.

I pushed through the glass door, which had jammed slightly as long as I had known it, dumped my briefcase on to a stool by the counter and sat on the next one.

'Afternoon, Mr Tyroll,' said the larger of the two counter-hands, moving along to my position. 'Been potted again, have you?'

I smiled, ruefully. 'Two hundred and fifty pounds for obstructing Edward Street with a caravan,' I reported. 'It would do Edward Street good if they bombed it! A tea and two buttered Chelseas, please, Ruby.'

She turned to pick up the huge brown teapot. 'You defending that Darren Gormley?' she asked over her shoulder. 'The rapist?' Pouring tea expertly with one hand, she nonchalantly wielded a pair of plastic tongs with the other, transferring two Chelsea buns from a display case on to a plate.

'Yes,' I said, 'and he isn't a rapist.'

'Why's he been charged, then?' she demanded.

11

'Because', I said, 'he had the misfortune to fall into Inspector Saffary's hands at the wrong time.'

'Oh, that Saffary,' she said, pushing the plate and cup across. 'You know what they calls him, don't you?'

I shook my head.

'They calls him "The Tailor" 'cos they reckon he stitches people up proper. I hope your fellow's guilty if Saffary's got his knife into him,' and she chuckled, wheezily.

'Thanks,' I said. 'I don't just come in here for the tea and buns, it's because you cheer me up.'

As I paid her and left the counter, balancing plate and cup in one hand, briefcase in the other, she called after me, 'Dr Mac's down the back. He'll cheer you up. Always got a funny story about dead people's bits and innards, he has.'

Macintyre looked up as I approached his table. 'Ah!' he exclaimed. 'Fresh from defending the wrongdoer and punishing the children of the rich – how are you, Christopher?'

I dumped my burdens and slid into a seat opposite the doctor. 'Not in a mood for your raillery, Doc. Ruby says you'll cheer me up with a funny story about the innards of dead bodies.'

'Funny peculiar or funny ha-ha?' asked the Scotsman.

'Either'll do,' I said, sipping my tea.

'Well, peculiar then,' said the pathologist. 'One of your clients became one of mine this morning.'

'That's not peculiar. Most of my clients live round here, some of them die round here, and you get to pick over the remains of any unusual deaths. Who was it?'

'You make me sound like a carrion bird,' complained the doctor. 'It was an old man called Brown, lived across by the park.'

'Not really a client. I bought his house for him and made his will, that's all. I don't think he liked me very much. The first time he came to my office he said, "You're the fellow that defends gypsies, aren't you?" When I admitted my follies he said, "Can't stand 'em myself – a dirty, shiftless lot, but they're getting a hard time since that stupid Act and someone's got to stand up for them. That's why I came here. I want someone who'll stand up if the going gets tough." After which tribute he allowed me to draw his will and buy his house, but you'll understand that we never exactly socialised.'

'What going?' asked Mac.

'What "What going"?'

'Why did he think the going was going to get tough?'

'I've no idea,' I said. 'Perhaps it was just a form of words. Why do you ask?'

'Because he's dead, laddie.'

I took another long draught of tea. 'How did he die?' I asked.

'I thought you'd never ask,' said Macintyre. 'He was mugged, or so it seems.'

'Mugged?'

'Aye. Apparently he used to walk round the lake in the park every morning as a constitutional. This morning somebody mugged him. Mother and kiddie going to feed the ducks saw his feet sticking out under the bushes.'

I shook my head. 'That's terrible. He must have been eighty or more. What a way to end!'

'Aye,' said the doctor. 'He was a big old fellow, put up one hell of a scrap.'

'Did he?'

'Oh yes. Bruises and knuckle abrasions – he must have landed a punch or two – and his walking-stick had blood and tissue on it that wasnae his.'

'What killed him?'

'That's one of the funny things,' said Macintyre. 'He was battered all right, and it looked like someone had had gloved hands on his throat, but the actual cause of death was a single blow to the neck.'

'A karate chop?'

'Aye, that kind of thing.' The pathologist leaned across and took my second Chelsea bun, attacking it with relish. 'That's all this town needs – Ninja muggers in the park!'

'Be my guest,' said I. 'Do you really think it was an Oriental?'

'No. If anyone asked my opinion, based on the body, I'd say the police should be seeking a tall, young, strong man, with brown hair, wearing soft footwear and sporting a fresh injury and maybe bloodstained clothing. Possibly an ex-soldier or a martial arts practitioner.'

'Why tall, brown-haired and soft-shoed?' I asked.

'Ah, Watson, Watson!' exclaimed the Scot. 'Tall, because ye cannae easily strangle anyone who's much taller than you, but someone tried to strangle the old fellow and he was six foot two. Brown-haired, because he took a clout on the head from the walking-stick and left hair and blood behind. With soft shoes, because he attacked from behind, which means he came up quietly on the gravel path by the lake.'

'Brilliant, Holmes!' I said.

'Superintendent Howard didnae think so,' said Macintyre. 'He's got a completely different idea.' He called to the ladies at the counter, 'Ruby, June, have you got the afternoon paper?'

Ruby moved slowly down the café with it and gave it to him, folded inside out to expose the TV page. He turned it right way out and passed it across the table. I put down my cup and took in the front page headline:

OAP MURDERED IN PARK
Police Appeal For Witnesses

85-year-old Walter Brown, a retired local government official of Grenville Street, Belston, was found dead in the town's park early this morning.

Mr Brown, who made a practice of walking in the park as soon as it opened, had been murdered, apparently by a mugger. His watch and wallet were missing.

The body was found by Mrs Eileen Probert, 31, of Brean Walk. She had been taking her seven-year-old daughter, Dorothy, to feed the ducks in the park.

Mrs Probert told us: 'I was just breaking up the bread for the ducks when Dotty said that there was a man asleep in the bushes. Well, you do get drunks there in the summer, but when I looked I could see he was dead, so I called the police.'

Detective Superintendent Howard of Central Midlands Police said: 'This poor old man was savagely struck down

14

while enjoying a morning walk. We are looking for witnesses who may have seen anyone acting strangely in the vicinity of the park or the lake at about eight this morning.'

Police have issued a description of a man they want to interview. He is described as about 5' 10", dark-haired, unshaven and wearing a zip-up leather jacket and dark jeans or trousers.

I looked up from reading. 'So you've got an ex-soldier about six feet with brown hair and Howard's got a dark, scruffy, shorter bloke in leather jacket and jeans. Where did he get that from?'

'I dinna ken,' said Macintyre, 'but he's wrong.'

'You sound very sure of yourself.'

'Oh, I am, Chris, I am.' The doctor reached in his pocket and removed something. 'Have you heard of cadaveric spasm?' he asked.

'Of course I have. The famous "dead man's grip" beloved of novelists, when the hand of a dying person stays locked around something they were holding as they died.'

'Aye, that's the one. Dosnae happen so often as novelists wish, but it happened to old Brown this morning.'

'And what had he got hold of? The mugger's business card?'

'That,' said Macintyre, and dropped something on the table. It rolled erratically towards me.

I picked it up. It was a brown button.

'It's a button,' I said. 'Zip-up leather jackets don't have buttons.'

Macintyre smiled. 'Half marks, laddie. It didnae come off a leather jacket, that's true, but what kind of jacket did it come off?'

I looked again at the button, rolling it in my hand.

'It's moulded plastic,' I said. 'No – it's woven brown leather!' I looked up in surprise.

'Aye,' said the pathologist, triumphantly. 'It's the kind of button you get when you pay too much for your clothes. Nowadays even expensive clothes have plastic imitations, but our mugger wears the real, hideously expensive, thing.'

'What did Howard say about it?'

'He said it wasnae important and would I kindly confine my report to injuries and cause of death. What's more, he hasnae asked me yet to get a DNA check on the tissue from Brown's walking-stick.'

He drank noisily from his mug of tea. 'Something stinks, laddie, something stinks.'

Down at the other end of the café the ancient wall-phone rang. 'That'll be Jayne, looking for me,' I said, and gulped the rest of my tea.

'Mr Tyroll,' called Ruby, 'that was your office. Jayne says you've got an important foreign client waiting.'

'D'ye train her to broadcast these lies for advertising purposes?' asked Macintyre.

'Jayne', I muttered, 'would claim that the entire Cabinet were in the waiting-room if it interfered with my tea-break.'

2

My office is in a distinguished Victorian building, across the square from the Guildhall, distinguished mainly by the imperial statuary in terracotta on the front and the poor state of decoration. A brass plate at the building's side entrance bears the name and a long flight of stairs leads up to the reception window. In the days before street-corner betting shops the office had been the chambers of a credit bookmaker. Perhaps that was why there was a discreet rear exit via a fire escape at the back of the building. I had been going to have it changed before I realised its advantages.

Now I walked through the front entrance, ignored the stairs, and carried on into the yard, mounting to my floor by the fire stairs. Like almost every working day I made a mental note to have them checked for rust and promptly forgot it.

Jayne was my secretary when I occupied one room and shared it with the clatter of her old-fashioned Underwood. Ten years on she sits in state at an antique oak desk bigger than my own, from whence she runs the office's administration and much of my private life. Now she regarded me with impatience as I put my head around her door.

'Do you think', she asked, 'that, before you settle down to a disgusting-stories session with old Macintyre in the Rendez-vous, you could remember to call in?'

'Tried to,' I lied, 'but the phones were all busy. National press phoning the Murphy result to London – hold the front page and all that.'

She eyed me hard and silently and jotted a note on a pad.

'What's that? You're not keeping a list of my excuses, are you?'

'That', she said, 'was a note for the next office meeting re the purchase of a mobile phone.'

'Staff wouldn't stand for it,' I assured her. 'Health and Safety, that kind of thing. They fry your brains, you know.'

'I don't believe a word of it,' she said.

'You should. It was in the papers. Must be true. They don't put lies in newspapers. Anyway, it's no worse than important international clients at half-past four on a Tuesday. Is Alasdair in? I want to talk to him about Gormley's committal.'

'He's still in Brum,' she said, 'and you've still got a client.'

She picked up a business card from her desk and gave it to me. It said:

> Dr Sheila McKenna,
> Dept. of Social History,
> University of Adelaide,
> South Australia.

'She's been waiting half an hour,' Jayne said. 'She said she had to see you and you would know what it was about.'

'Well, I don't,' I said. 'And I can think of better ways to end a bad day than being nice to some sun-raddled old academic biddy in a hideous print dress and elastic stockings, with an accent like a sawmill at full stretch.'

'Lost Murphy's case, did you?' she said, brightly. 'I'll give you five minutes to make your desk presentable, then I'll wheel her in, elastic stockings and all,' and she looked at her watch meaningfully.

I gave way. 'OK,' I said, wearily. 'Set some tea and biscuits up, will you? They say that Adelaide's so respectable you can get arrested for walking down the street with your gloves off after dark, so we'd better do the posh Pommy professional bit.'

The tea was on my desk three minutes later. Two minutes afterwards a brisk rap announced Jayne with the client.

No elastic stockings, no print dress, no sun-raddled complexion. No old biddy, either. Dr McKenna was a lightly suntanned, tall blonde of about thirty. Her natural linen safari suit was cut close enough to reveal a lithe, well-modelled figure and under the fringe of her ash-blonde hair a pair of grey-blue eyes looked out wide and direct from a fringe of freckles.

I rose and motioned her to a chair, realising that, whatever her business, the day was looking up. 'Please have a seat, doctor. I'm Christopher Tyroll.'

I had been wrong about the voice as well. It was rich and soft and its accent only made it more attractive. 'Please don't call me "doctor",' she said. 'It makes me sound like some kind of sawbones. You can call me Sheila if you don't make obvious Pommy jokes about it.'

'Right, right.' I cleared my throat. 'I'm Christopher – Chris. You told my secretary that your business was with me and I would know what it was.'

'That's right.'

'I'm sorry to say that I don't. Do you have the right firm, doc – Sheila?'

She drew a paper from a plain leather shoulder-bag. 'No doubt at all. This is Tyrolls, 24a Jubilee Chambers, isn't it?'

'Well, yes, but . . .'

'Perhaps I should tell you what my connection with Belston is,' she continued. 'My people came from here. My mother was Patricia Brown and my grandfather is Walter Brown of Grenville Street. You're his solicitor, aren't you?'

It had to be a dreadful coincidence. She couldn't possibly have had time to hear of the old man's death and make her way from South Australia. So she didn't know – and now I had to tell her.

I picked up the teapot. 'That's right,' I said slowly. 'Would you care for tea?'

She let me pour the Earl Grey and took it without milk. When we had both sipped I said, 'Have you seen your grandfather lately, Sheila?'

She shook her head. 'Not for five years,' she said, 'but we kept in touch. He was my only relative. My mum and dad emigrated in the fifties, but they were both killed in a crash on the Eyre Highway five years ago, so Grandpa's all I've got.'

I pushed the biscuits across, fumbling for words. 'You came straight here today?' I asked.

'No,' she said. 'I'd had to replace a colleague at a conference in Brussels at short notice, so I booked some leave and decided to surprise the old boy. The conference finished this morning, so I came over, but he wasn't home this afternoon. The only thing I knew was that you're his lawyer, so I thought I'd better come here.'

I still hadn't nerved myself to break the news when the phone rang. Gratefully, I excused myself and picked it up. Jayne was on the other end.

'I'm sorry to interrupt you, but I think it's connected. I've got Sergeant Parry on the phone. He wants to talk about Mr Brown's death and he's mentioned a Dr McKenna.'

'OK Jayne. Put him through.'

Parry's cheery Welsh voice came on. 'Hello, Chris. You'll have read about the mugging in the park this morning? One of yours, I believe?'

'That's right.'

'Well, we need to get into his house and we need to contact any relatives. Now his housekeeper's got keys, so we're going in now, but she says his only relative was a Dr McKenna at Adelaide University in Aussie. We've rung there, but they say she's on leave in the UK. You wouldn't know where we could contact her, would you?'

'Yes,' I said. 'Right here.' I dared not give Sheila an inkling of the conversation's content.

19

'Right there? You don't mean in your office?'

'That's right.'

Suddenly it dawned on Parry. 'She's with you now, isn't she? Does she know?'

'Yes, and no.'

'Jesus, Chris! I'm sorry, man. I'd no idea. I'd better leave you to it.' He paused. 'Look, when she's ready I'll need to talk to her, OK?'

'Yes, that'll be OK in due course. I'll let you know, John. 'Bye.'

When I put the phone down I knew that my evasions had run out. I had kept the phone close to my ear. She couldn't have heard, but she knew. She was watching me, sharply.

'Was that about my grandfather?' she asked.

'Yes,' I said, 'and about you. The local police want to talk to you.'

'What's happened? Has something happened to Grandpa?'

I twisted a ballpen between my hands. 'There's no way to wrap this up,' I said. 'Your grandfather was found dead this morning, in the park. I'm sorry.'

She jerked her face away from me as though she had been slapped, and kept it averted while she fought down the reaction. When she turned back her eyes were moist but she was in control.

'He was eighty-five,' she said. 'I guess it had to happen soon. That's why I wanted to see him.'

'It wasn't his age,' I said. 'He was attacked – mugged. He was . . .'

'Murdered?' she said, quietly.

'Yes, I'm afraid he was. Look, Sheila, I don't know what your business was with me, but I'm sure it can wait.'

She shook her head. 'No, it can't. I didn't just come to see him. He wrote me a letter, a very strange letter. He told me to see you. It worried me a bit.'

She took a couple of folded sheets out of her bag and passed them across. I recognised my former client's firm, even hand, the writing of a man who had been taught properly and had never forgotten.

'Read it,' she said. 'You might know what he meant.'

I skimmed the letter quickly. It was not very long:

My dear Sheila,

It seems to be a long time since you have been home, and I am not getting any younger. If you could find the time to come over soon, I would be very glad to see you.

When you get to my age, you start looking back, and I have been trying to set a few things in order before I go. I suppose some people wouldn't think they were important, but I was brought up to do what was right.

There is one matter in particular that has bothered me for a long time, but now I think I might have the answer. I'd just like to see right done before I go, but I don't know if I shall be able to finish it off. That's why I should like to talk to you about it.

If you can't come soon, if I'm gone before you come home, go and see my solicitor. His name is Christopher Tyroll, of Tyrolls, 24a Jubilee Buildings. That's in the Market Place, opposite the Guildhall. He's a bit of an odd fellow for a lawyer, but I think that he likes to do things right in his own way. He'll help you if I'm not here, but I hope I shall be.

In the hope of seeing you soon,

Your loving Grandpa

P.S. Don't worry about the cost. If you can come I'll buy the ticket.

'I can see why it worried you,' I said. 'So far as I could see, he wasn't a man who dwelt much on the past, nor did he seem unduly worried about the future. He made a will, of course, and we'll have to go over that. Basically, he left everything to you apart from a small bequest to his housekeeper. It won't keep you in luxury, but he was a careful man and, apart from the house, there's a decent sum as well.'

She waved my talk of the will aside, impatiently. 'That can wait,' she said. 'What was it that he was trying to sort out? What is it that you can help me with?'

21

'That's a bit of a problem,' I admitted. 'I haven't got the least idea what this letter's about.'

3

She stared at me. 'You haven't the least idea?' she repeated. 'Really?'

'Really, Sheila. As I said, he came in a couple of years ago and said he wanted to exercise an option to purchase on his house. That was no problem, he paid cash in full. Then he wanted a will made. That was straightforward, too. He left everything to you apart from a few hundred to Mrs Croft, his housekeeper. I must have seen him about half a dozen times at most and that was just business. He never mentioned any problem to me, or discussed any proposition with me, other than the house and the will.'

'When did you see him last?' she asked. She picked up the letter. 'This is dated about six weeks ago. Perhaps he intended to see you about something and didn't.'

I picked up the phone. 'Jayne,' I asked, 'can you check the last time I saw Walter Brown? Yes, I know it's all on the computer, but I hate looking like an idiot in front of a client when I press the wrong button. And can you bring in his house file and the will file? Thanks.'

I turned back to my visitor. 'I doubt that they'll tell us much,' I said. 'He was a pleasure to deal with because he knew what he wanted, he answered letters and he paid his bill promptly. There'll be nothing additional in those files.'

Jayne tapped the door and entered with two folders. Placing them on my desk, she gave me a slip of paper. 'That's all his appointments with you about the house and the will. On the last date you didn't see him.'

I glanced over the slip. 'What happened that time?' I asked.

'You were at court. He came in without an appointment and said he'd mislaid his copy of the will and he'd like to look at

22

ours. I took ours out of the deeds cabinet and let him read it and he went away. That's all.'

'Thanks, Jayne,' I said and she left. I picked up the two slim folders and skimmed through them quickly. 'No, there's nothing here apart from correspondence about the house and the will.' I took a photocopy from one folder and passed it across to her. 'There's a copy of his will for you.'

She glanced at it briefly then folded it into her bag. 'Disappointing.' She smiled. 'I thought you were going to sit at a long table and read it all out to me and Mrs Whatsername.'

I was pleased to see her smiling. 'Obviously you get bad American movies in Australia, as well,' I said. 'What's the date on your grandfather's letter?'

She picked it up from the desk again. 'It's 14th April, just over six weeks ago.'

'That's funny,' I said. 'That's the day before he came in here to look at his will.'

'Is that unusual?' she asked. 'People forgetting what's in their will?'

'Well, sometimes they think of things afterwards. They can't remember if they put Cousin Ethel in and they can't find their copy because they hid it away safely, so they come in and ask. I shouldn't have thought your grandfather would do that. Apart from the will being so simple, he always struck me as better organised than that.'

'He was,' she said. 'It's not like him at all. He was like an elephant – he never forgot anything. He never mislaid anything, either. He was in local government offices all his life and he was a fanatic about keeping records and keeping things in their proper places.'

An idea occurred to me. 'So, if he hadn't really forgotten,' I said, 'then he came in here to talk to me about something he wouldn't tell Jayne.'

'You've lost me,' she said.

'The bit about the will was an excuse. He wanted to talk to me, but I was out, so he made an excuse for being here. That's odd in itself.'

'Why?'

23

'Because Jayne may frighten the hell out of me, and she can empty a waiting-room full of lager louts with one stamp of her jackboots, but the older clients think she's wonderful. I wonder why he wouldn't tell her.'

Sheila looked at her watch. 'We're getting nowhere,' she said, 'and I'm taking up your time. Look, I've got to fix up to stay somewhere, but when I've done that I'm going to stay around a while. Can we come back on this?'

'Of course,' I said, delighted that she was staying, even if only briefly. 'Look, the Victoria, across the square, is about as good as you'll find around here. Let me take you across and see you settled in and – if it's not the wrong time – let me buy you dinner tonight?'

She smiled, warmly. 'No, I – it's not the wrong time at all. I'd be delighted.'

I try hard to avoid male arrogance, but you need to try harder than that when you sit in the restaurant of the town's biggest hotel and a head-turningly lovely blonde is escorted to your table. Even more so when the other diners know you, but they've never seen her before. Throughout the meal a succession of professional colleagues, professional enemies, and slight acquaintances paused at our table to say hello and be introduced to my guest. To each one I explained Sheila as 'Dr McKenna, a client from Australia'.

During a lull in the traffic she said, 'You seem to be a pretty popular bloke, Chris.'

'Don't you believe it. They're all going back to their tables and saying to each other, "What's that bloody commie Tyroll doing with a beautiful client from Australia?"'

'Are you really a communist?' she asked, wide-eyed. 'I thought they all gave up when the Soviet Union folded.'

'I'm not anything. I've never belonged to a political party in my life, but I was brought up by a mum who taught me a few simple, obvious ideas like equality before the law and so on. Try and practise that in England and it upsets a lot of people.'

She turned her wineglass, thoughtfully. 'Grandpa was a socialist,' she said. 'Perhaps that's why he thought well of you.'

24

'We don't have socialists in England any more. They call them "old Labour" now, but I don't think that would have worried your grandfather.'

'No,' she said. 'He used to say, "Just make up your mind what's right, my girl, and don't let anyone mess you about."'

I raised my own glass. 'Here's to him,' I said, and she lifted her own in acknowledgement.

We had finished dinner and removed to the coffee lounge when Macintyre tracked us down. 'Chris,' he trumpeted from the doorway, 'the jealous drunkards in the front bar tell me you are playing host to a beautiful foreigner.'

I groaned inwardly, fearing some indiscretion from Mac relating to the day's post-mortem. Quickly I said, 'Meet Dr McKenna, Mac. She's the granddaughter of Walter Brown who died this morning.'

'Not, I hope, a medical doctor,' said Macintyre, taking Sheila's proffered hand. 'I don't think I could stand the competition.'

'No worries,' she said. 'I'm a social historian, not a real doctor, Mac. And the name's Sheila and we'll have less of the foreigner bit. I'm pure Belston on both sides of the family.'

Macintyre dropped into a chair. 'I'm sorry for your bad news,' he said.

'Grandfather was an old man, Mac. He can't have had long.'

'No, surely, but it's not the way an old man should go.' The doctor beckoned a passing waiter and ordered drinks. When the waiter had gone he asked, 'Did you tell Sheila about the button?'

'The button? What button?' she asked.

'I'm sorry,' I said. 'I'd only just heard of your grandfather's death when I came back to the office. Finding you there and puzzling about the letter drove it out of my head. You tell Sheila, Mac.'

'Do you mind if I discuss a physical phenomenon in the dead?' asked Macintyre, with unwonted delicacy.

'You carry on, Mac. I'm not going to cry Ruth all over the table. I want to know what your button is about.'

'Does cadaveric spasm mean anything to you?' asked the Scotsman.

25

'Yes,' she said. 'We've got a song about it in Aussie.'

He was wide-eyed. 'A song, you say? About cadaveric spasm?'

'Sure,' she said. '"Gallant Peter Clarke" – Clarke was bailed up by a bushranger and fought with him. The bushranger killed Clarke, but Clarke had his throat in a grip and never let go when he died. Hours later they found the killer still trying to get away. So the song says.'

'That's not in Camp's *Forensic Medicine*,' said the pathologist, as though it should be, and I grinned to see Macintyre so completely upstaged. 'Still,' he went on, 'you want to hear about the button.'

He outlined his theories quickly and clearly. Sheila's expression grew more perplexed. The drinks were served and, when Mac had finished his explanation, she sipped at hers thoughtfully for a while.

'Let's get this right,' she said, eventually. 'You think that the man in the leather jacket had nothing to do with Grandpa's death?'

'That's not what I said,' replied the doctor. 'He might have done. I believe the police got his description from the park-keeper, who saw him hanging about outside when he unlocked the gates this morning. What I am saying is that that was not the man your grandfather was struggling with when he died.'

'And Grandpa was killed by a skilled karate blow?'

'Aye, an expert blow.'

'And the police are ignoring what you have told them?'

'So it would seem.'

'Then what the hell's going on? Do your police often ignore evidence in murder cases?'

'Sometimes,' said Macintyre. 'Sometimes.'

'And what times are those?' Sheila demanded sharply.

'Usually when the funnies are involved.'

'The funnies?' She looked bewildered.

'The security services,' I explained. 'DI5 or 6 or 9 or one of those.'

Sheila's jaw dropped. She looked from me to the pathologist.

26

'Are you saying', she said slowly, 'that poor old Grandpa was killed by a government agent?'

'Something like that, lassie. Something like that.'

4

'That's crazy!' she said. 'I'm sorry, Mac, but that's ab-so-lutely crazy.'

'Aye,' he said, soberly, 'it is, but it may be something like the truth, nevertheless.'

I was watching the old doctor and cursing him silently. 'Aren't you pushing it a bit?' I said.

'I wish I was, but we've both heard the stories of cases that the police don't want to look into, or that they won't look into because someone has told them not to. Remember the lady who grew roses over in Shropshire? That was never solved, was it? They say she was killed by a private security firm employed by one of the funny departments. And yon fellow who was shot by the SAS up north – the fellow who killed a copper who caught him hanging about a government transmitter? They even took away the newspapermen's films of the shooting. You can believe me or not, but I know they kill. I've been in my business a good few years and sometimes you get the scent of something that isnae as it should be.'

I knew he was right, but I didn't want him to be. 'I thought one Prime Minister asked the secret service to put down Idi Amin and they said they had "no facility",' I remarked.

Mac stared at me. 'Well, they would say that, wouldn't they? Believe you me, Chris, they'll kill when it suits them.'

He hauled himself out of his chair. 'I'm an old man,' he said, 'and maybe I've had a drop too much. I shouldnae be upsetting you, Sheila. Goodnight to you both,' and he ambled away.

Sheila watched him go. 'Is he for real?' she asked.

'It's not my business to upset you, either, but for all his

professional Scotsman act, Hector Macintyre is a damned good forensic pathologist. I've had occasion in the past to regret not listening to his advice.'

She shook her head slowly from side to side. 'I can't handle this. My grandpa gets mugged and murdered and I've got a lawyer and a pathologist saying that the government did it! Why would they?'

I couldn't answer that one. I set my glass down. 'I never really knew your grandfather,' I said. 'What was he like? What had he been?'

'He was the first of his family to wear a white collar,' she said. 'His people were miners, but he left school and went into an office, a land agent, I think. Then he went into the Town Hall. He was forty-five years in local government. Retired with a gold watch.'

'What did he do in retirement? Did he have any hobbies?'

'Oh, sure. He walked miles and he read. History mostly, political, social, local. I came over five years ago, when my parents were killed, and we spent the whole time walking. We visited every historic site for miles and he was faster up and down hills than I was.'

'And his mind?'

'His mind?' she echoed. 'Oh, the letter – no, he wasn't going daffy five years ago and it didn't look like it from his letters. You saw him more recently, what did you think?'

I remembered the tall, upright old man who never wasted a word and I shook my head. 'No,' I said. 'There was nothing daffy about your grandfather. He was a pleasure to deal with. Completely lucid and straightforward.'

'That was Grandpa,' she said. 'If he thought something ought to be done then he did it.'

'Didn't that attitude make him enemies?'

'Not really. I think he was pretty good at his job and even those who didn't like his politics had to admit that.'

I sank into silence. After a few moments I said, 'You didn't mention the forces. Was he ever in the services?'

'No,' she said. 'He was a pacifist before the war, but the

Nazis convinced him. He wanted to fight, but he was in a whatchermecally . . .'

'A reserved occupation?'

'That's right. Having changed his outlook he was pretty peeved that they thought he was better at pushing paper.'

I stared into my glass. 'I have to agree with you – Mac's theories don't make sense. There doesn't seem to be any reason for it to be more than a mugging.'

'Not unless he was killed because he knew the secrets of the ring road contracts in 1948.'

'There wasn't any ring road in 1948.' I grinned. 'They planned one in 1938, abandoned it during the war, built the first half in 1958, and they've just announced that they're not going to finish it.'

She grinned. 'Grandpa would have been furious,' she said.

After another round of drinks I paid the bill and she walked with me to the lobby.

'Thanks for tonight, Chris,' she said.

I was embarrassed. 'Look,' I said, 'I owe you an apology. I invited you for dinner to try and keep your mind off things and we've spent half the evening talking about those things.'

'No worries,' she said. 'When the time comes I'm going to fold up and howl like a baby, but right now I want to know why my grandpa died. I'm just grateful you didn't leave me alone in a strange town to start howling.'

'I've got no court appearances tomorrow,' I said. 'There are formalities. You'll have to identify your grandfather and Sergeant Parry will want to talk to you. I'll pick you up here at ten and we can arrange it.'

There were cabs on the rank outside the Victoria, but it was a warm night. I decided to walk home while I pondered on Sheila, her grandfather and Doc Macintyre's theories.

My home is a Victorian villa in Whitegate Village, on the far side of a hill from the town centre. Without hurrying I soon covered the mile or so of main street that led to the Village, and turned into the old, winding streets of an area that had

29

remained remarkably unchanged since it really was a village. One of the reasons I live there is the Village's tree-lined streets and alleys and now the lamplight shone through the leaves, casting a green glow on the narrow pavements.

The pondering wasn't going very well. Somehow it kept being distracted by recollections of a pair of grey eyes with freckles underneath. I'd hardly looked at a woman seriously since my marriage broke up, largely because I'd been too busy and anyway you're not supposed to mess with lady clients. That can end up putting you in front of a board of hatchet-men in a Masonic Temple in Carey Street who just know that you're not fit to grace the legal profession. Now I'd been smitten by a transient Australian. As I walked down the steeply sloping street on which I live I passed a parked car in which a dark huddle in the front seats suggested that someone else was harbouring romantic thoughts.

I had almost reached my gate when a slight noise drew my attention. Close behind me a car engine had coughed quietly into life.

Surprised by the sound, I turned, straight into a pair of powerful headlights that had just been switched on. I was dazzled by the glare but I knew the car was almost on top of me. It had rolled silently down the slope after I passed and was now coming at me under power.

As the vehicle mounted the pavement, I grabbed wildly and unseeingly for the top of the gate and sprang upwards as hard as I could. It was not hard enough. The top of the iron gate raked my leg painfully as I rolled across it, but I dropped inside it just as the car flashed across the gateway, scraping the wall alongside.

I lay on my own front path, gasping for breath and feeling the blood beginning to seep along my grazed shin. It hurt like hell and I was too winded to pick myself up. If they came out of the car at me, they'd got me. Then I heard it accelerate away down the hill. When its note faded I climbed cautiously to my feet and let myself in through the front door. With a torch from the house I limped back into the lane. The weather had been dry for days and there were no tyre-marks that I could distinguish, but I did find the scatter of dirt from the underbody where the car had mounted the kerb in its last swing towards me and on the right side of the gate there were streaks of blue enamel on the brickwork.

Indoors again I took a careful, wincing shower and dressed the long scrape that the gate's top had left on my leg. Then I lay in bed and wondered. Had someone really just tried to kill me?

5

The first moves in the morning were painful. Apart from the scraped injury down my left leg, the limb's abused muscles had stiffened in the night. Even a long hot shower effected only a slight improvement and I was forced to take a cab into the town. In the bright summer morning I found it even harder to believe that someone had set out to kill or maim me at my own gate on the previous night.

Sheila was waiting for me at the Victoria, and I let the cabbie fetch her and take us across to the office. I limped painfully up the stairs behind her and, over coffee, phoned Detective Sergeant Parry.

When I put the phone down I said, 'Right, John Parry wants you to make a formal identification. Would you like me to come with you – for moral support?'

She shook her head. 'No thanks,' she said. 'He was my grandpa, we were each other's only family. I'd like to do it on my own.'

'I was only thinking – ' I began, but she interrupted.

'Five years ago I had to identify my parents. They went off the Eyre Highway and they'd lain in the sun before I saw them. I shall be all right.'

I let her go and sat leafing again through Walter Brown's two files. Eventually I flung them into the out-tray with a grunt of impatience.

Jayne put her head round the door to say that Sheila was back, together with Sergeant Parry.

'What's this I hear', Jayne asked, 'about you dining at the Victoria last night with your sun-raddled old academic biddy? Client relations, was it?'

'Have you really nothing better to do than gossip about my private life?' I asked.

'Me? Gossip?' she exclaimed, wide-eyed, with an innocent hand pressed to her chest. 'Everybody I've spoken to this morning from the magistrates' clerk to the window-cleaner mentioned it. Good job I didn't tell them that you came in stiff and limping!'

'Just show them in and let us have more coffee,' I said, knowing that I was losing.

The big Welsh sergeant ushered Sheila into the room. 'Morning, Chris,' he said. 'I've explained to Dr McKenna – Sheila – that I'll have to take a statement from her as to what she knew about Mr Brown.'

'Not much that'll help you, sergeant,' she said.

'Nevertheless,' he said, 'it's got to be done. Usual procedures and all that.'

He unzipped his document case and spread statement forms on the desk, beginning to fill in the headings on one in his neat, even script.

The exercise did not take long and I learned nothing new. When Sheila had signed the forms, Parry slid them into his briefcase and stood up.

'Thank you,' he said to Sheila. 'I don't suppose we'll need to bother you again unless something comes up, but can we contact you here?'

'Until further notice you'll find me here or at the Victoria, yes. Tell me, sergeant, how long do you expect this to take?'

'How long?' he repeated.

'Yes,' she said. 'How long before you nail the scumbag that killed my grandfather?'

He shook his head. 'No way of telling, really. We've got the description I told you about, but it's not much of a help. Lot of blokes in Belston would meet that description, and maybe he doesn't come from here.'

She looked him squarely in the eye. 'You're talking about the man the park-keeper saw, the man in the black leather zipper jacket?'

'Yes,' he said. 'That's all we've got at present.'

'What about', she said slowly, 'the leather button in Grandpa's fist?'

Parry looked at her blankly, and I could see that the sergeant really didn't know what she meant.

'You'd better sit down again, John. It sounds like someone's been keeping things from you,' I said.

Parry lowered himself back into his chair, looking from me to Sheila for enlightenment.

'Have you talked to Dr Mac?' I asked.

'No,' he replied. 'Howard dealt with that himself. Gave me the report when he assigned me. Why?'

Quickly I outlined Macintyre's information and theories. As I talked Parry's face set harder.

'I knew nothing of this,' he said at the end. 'Howard gave me a summary of Mac's report. Never mentioned a button. When I saw the cause of death and suggested an ex-soldier Howard pooh-poohed it. Said a martial arts freak was more likely.'

'And what difference does it make?' asked Sheila.

'It makes it difficult,' said the detective. 'If my super's playing about with the funnies, it'll make it bloody difficult. Still – difficult isn't impossible.'

He stood up again and I asked, 'Did you bring the keys to the house?'

'Yes.' Sergeant Parry delved into his document case and brought out a small bunch of keys and a form. 'You'll have to sign for them,' he said.

I scribbled a signature and took the keys. 'I take it we can go to the house when we like? Your boys have done with it?'

'Nothing there for them,' said Parry. 'A place for everything and everything in its place, all beautifully dusted and polished by Mrs Croft. Nothing to help us. You're welcome to it, but if you come across anything we missed give me a shout.'

When the detective was gone I called a cab. 'No time like the present,' I told Sheila. 'Let's go and look at the house.'

Walter Brown's home in Grenville Street was late Victorian, standing at the left-hand end of a terrace on the slope above the park. At the front a small lawn lay behind a low wall, and a path at the side led to the front door and carried on to the rear of the house.

We stood on the steps and I tried all three of the Yale keys on the ring. One of them turned in the lock, but the door remained locked.

'Funny,' I thought aloud. 'Parry's men wouldn't have dropped the catch. Let's go round the back.'

We followed the path along the side of the house and turned into the rear yard. I saw it at once – a square hole cut in the frosted glass of the back door.

'Go next door,' I told her, 'and phone John Parry. Tell him your grandfather's place has been burgled.' I gave her the phone number. 'I'll be in the garden,' I said.

As Sheila went on her errand I limped across the path between the yard and the back garden. The garden was all lawn, overhung by two mature trees at the far corners. I sat on a seat under one of the trees and lit a cigarette. While I waited for Sheila I turned the case over in my mind.

A retired local government officer in his eighties who lives alone and writes a strange letter to his only living relative, then gets killed while strolling in the park by a killer with an expensive taste in sports coats. A meaningless description circulated by the police and a detective superintendent who keeps information from the officer in charge in the case. A burglary at the dead man's home and perhaps – perhaps – an attempt on the victim's lawyer last night. I churned it all backwards and forwards, but it kept bringing me back to the same point – the point where I couldn't make sense of any of it.

Sheila returned and sat beside me, silently. Minutes later Parry appeared round the side of the house with two younger officers. He came over to us.

34

'Haven't been inside, have you?' he asked.

'No,' I said. 'I thought there was something funny when none of the keys would open the front door, then I saw the hole in the back door.'

Parry turned and looked. 'Cut,' he said. 'There's tidy, isn't it?'

He moved down the garden towards the house and Sheila rose to follow him, but I pulled her back down to the seat.

'Leave it till the cops have finished,' I said. 'There could be a real mess in there and it'll only upset you.'

We sat, silent again, until Sergeant Parry came out to us.

'What's it like?' I asked him.

'I told you,' he said, 'it's tidy. In fact it's the neatest, tidiest bloody house-breaking I ever did see. Would you know if something was missing, Sheila?'

'I don't know,' she said. 'I suppose if it was something important I might.'

'Well, come and look then,' said Parry, and shepherded us down to the back door.

I had bought and sold dozens of houses similar to the old man's. I knew the agents' description by heart – 'Ground floor: hall, two sitting-rooms, dining-room and kitchen; First floor: three bedrooms, bathroom and boxroom.'

The back door gave on to the kitchen. There was no sign of disorder there. Even the piece cut from the pane in the door was missing. Next was a small breakfast room, set out with dining-table and chairs. Again there was no sign of disturbance. Parry bypassed the middle room and took us into the front sitting-room, where a wide bay window looked out on to the street. The three-piece suite and coffee table seemed in order and, more to the point, a thirty-inch colour television stood on a cabinet in the corner with a video-recorder underneath it.

'Are you sure someone came in?' I asked. 'The telly and the video are still here.'

'Oh yes, I'm sure,' said Parry. 'They weren't looking for tellies and videos, but they were looking for something. Come next door.'

He took us into the middle room, a smaller room with french

35

windows looking on to the back yard. It was lined with books and an old roll-topped desk with its lid pushed up stood in the right-hand corner by the fireplace.

'D'you see anything amiss, Sheila?' asked Parry.

'Yes,' she said. 'I do. They've been at the bookshelves. All the books are standing forward on the shelves. Gramps hated that. He always used to push them right back.'

Parry nodded. 'I saw this house yesterday afternoon,' he said. 'The books in here were all in order then. Soon as I came in today I knew someone had been through this room.'

'What were they looking for?' Sheila asked.

'If we knew that, we'd know a lot,' replied the detective. 'Can you spot anything missing?'

She stood in the middle of the room, looking about her, then walked to the bookshelves to the left of the fireplace. Running her hand along a shelf she came to a large red volume and pulled it out. She opened its cover and closed it again.

'I don't think they looked in the books,' she said. 'They must have pulled them out to look behind.'

'How do you know they didn't look inside?' asked Parry.

She laid the red volume on the desk and opened the cover again. 'Look,' she said. 'They don't seem to have disturbed that.'

It was not a book. It was a large tin box, its outside printed in colour to imitate a decorative red book-binding. Even the edges were gilded and marked with page lines.

'They gave them away with biscuits before the war,' she said. 'You were supposed to keep your jewellery and your insurance policies in them. When I came over as a kid Grandpa showed it to me and I thought it was wonderful.'

'What did he keep in it?' Parry asked.

'Just his personal mementoes, snapshots and things.' She reached into the box. 'And this,' she said, lifting something out. It was an old-fashioned gold watch. She held it up on its chain. 'Don't tell me somebody wouldn't have pocketed that if they'd seen it.'

'You could be right,' mused the detective. 'What else was in there?'

36

'Like I said – snapshots and stuff, souvenirs. I don't know altogether.'

'Will you take it,' he said, 'and have a look through it? Let me know if there's anything missing or odd in it, will you?'

His two assistants joined us. 'No luck, sarge,' said one. 'None of the neighbours heard or saw a thing, last night or this morning.' He looked around him. 'Do we know what they wanted?' he asked.

'God knows,' said Parry, gloomily, 'and he's not telling, is he?'

6

Back in the office Sheila sat and took out the contents of the tin box, one at a time, laying them along the edge of my desk.

There was the gold watch, with its inscription on the back – 'Presented to Walter Brown by the County Borough of Belston, for 45 years of loyal service.' Underneath it, still neatly folded in its envelope, was the letter from the Mayor which had accompanied the watch. There were insurance policies on the old man's life, the house and its contents, all premiums paid when due, and an airline's miniature 'Crossing the Line' certificate, dated about ten years before.

'When did he go abroad?' I asked.

'He flew out once to visit us,' Sheila said. 'Stayed for six weeks, but he didn't like it. "Too bloody casual altogether," he called us – not the family, Australia. He thought Adelaide was boring, all those straight streets. We went up to Ayers Rock, though, and he loved that.'

She went on laying out the contents of the tin. There was a postcard view of Ayers Rock, lit by the red glow at sunset with black desert all around, and a handful of colour snaps of the family by the Rock. An elastic band held together a small sheaf of letters in a childish hand and tucked into the band was a tie-pin. Set at its centre was a small opal with a tiny silver boomerang mounted across it. Sheila took it out and held it.

'We went to Cooberpedy,' she said, 'to see the opal mines. It was summer, and the temperature goes up to a hundred, but he always wore a tie – his union tie – and he always kept his shirtsleeves buttoned down. We used to rag him about it. I bought him this in the souvenir shop there.'

She clenched her hand tightly around the little pin and suddenly tears sprang in her eyes. She lowered her head and let them flow unchecked. I got up from the desk and moved behind her, touching her shoulder with my hand. Her free hand clasped mine.

'Don't go, Chris,' she said, and buried her face against me. I held her while she sobbed. Then, as quickly as it had begun, it was over. She pulled away and searched in her shoulder-bag for a tissue and a mirror.

When she had wiped her eyes she smiled at me. I was glad to see the brightness back in her eyes.

'Sorry,' she said. 'I thought I was a big tough Aussie, but I did warn you I'd howl eventually. I had planned to do it in private, though.'

'He meant a great deal to you,' I said.

'He did. It wasn't just that he was all I'd got. When we came here when I was a kid he was so good to me. I know my mother and father reckoned he could be awkward, but he was never anything but kind to me. He was a crusty, upright, decent, individualist old man, Chris, and he was the best grandfather anyone could want.'

She placed the tie-pin on the desk and I picked it up. 'You know some people think opal's an unlucky stone?' I said.

She nodded. 'But it shouldn't have been for him. He was a Capricorn. It was his birthstone.'

I picked up the phone and called Jayne. 'If you've still got your Birthdays Bottle in the bottom drawer, could you bring it in with a couple of glasses, please? No – purely medicinal.'

The drink brought colour back to Sheila's cheeks and she picked more snapshots out of the box. They were deckle-edged colour pictures of her parents and her around a Christmas tree

38

on a wooden verandah, Sheila in cap and gown at her gradua-
tion, Sheila in black and white, about ten years old in an English
garden. A bundle of membership cards in a rubber band
followed, cards going back before the war, recording dues paid
to the Labour Party and the National Association of Local
Government Officers. There was a solid metal badge, a crown
with ARP underneath it. She pushed it across the desk.

'Do you know what that is?' she asked. 'What's "ARP" stand
for?'

'"Air Raid Precautions" or "Air Raid Patrol". It's an air raid
warden's badge from the war,' I said, and turned it over in my
hand. 'He must have volunteered to go round shouting at
people who left chinks in their black-out,' I commented.

'How do you know?'

'The hallmark on the back means it's silver. They only gave
silver ones to people who volunteered. People who were
assigned got plain metal ones.'

She grinned. 'You Pommies are crazy,' she said. 'A world
war on and you handed out solid silver badges!'

'I wouldn't expect an Aussie Republican to understand the
fundamental importance of the distinction,' I said. 'One simply
has to keep the amateurs and the professionals apart – gentlemen and players, you know, that kind of thing. Once one allows
these distinctions to erode one loses all structure in society and
before you know it you'll have a barrow-boy as Lord Chancel-
lor. Anyway, we're not that stupid – giving the volunteers a
silver badge must have been a hell of a lot cheaper than paying
them!'

She grinned. 'Less of the Republican,' she said. 'I'm a loyal
citizen of the Commonwealth and subject of the Crown.
Grandpa wouldn't have let me grow up any other way. He was
a non-revolutionary socialist who believed in democratic mon-
archy. He used to say that presidents were just clapped-out
politicians on the make, that's why the Yanks keep shooting
theirs and the French keep changing them.'

She delved into the box again and showed me a copy of her
grandfather's will. 'I guess that answers one question,' she said.

Beneath the will were two cards and some buff booklets. The

cards bore a crown imprint and the booklets had a crown over the letters 'MofF' and a bold title, 'Ration Book'.

'Identity cards,' she said, holding up the cards, 'for himself and his wife, and ration books.' She put two of the books down and leafed through the third one. I picked up another and read the name inscribed in watered-down official ink on the cover.

'Who was James Brown?' I asked.

'Grandpa's brother – my Great-Uncle Jimmy. He lived in Nottingham and he died when I was about twelve. What's this?' she said, passing me another photograph.

It was a black and white, postcard-sized print, evidently pretty old. I peered at it, then took a magnifying glass from a drawer and examined it in more detail.

'There's no one I recognise in it,' Sheila said.

'It's fairly old,' I said. 'There's a group of blokes, seven of them, sitting and standing in a pub. 1940s, from the clothing. No women. A fellow on the left who didn't quite get into the shot. All the men around their twenties and thirties. No one who looks like your grandfather. Glasses raised, big smiles, right hands making V-signs.'

'You mean the international "Up yours" sign?'

'No, the Winston Churchill version the other way round – the Victory sign. No, wait a minute.'

I applied the lens again. 'One of them is giving it the usual way round.'

'What do you make of it?'

'Looks like a Victory party to me, VE Day or VJ Day, two fingers up, either way around, to Hitler and Co., a toast to victory.' I passed the photograph back.

She looked at it again. 'I wonder who they were,' she mused, 'and why he wasn't in it.'

'Perhaps he was behind the camera, or maybe that's his shoulder and knee at the edge. It looks like some of his contemporaries drinking to victory.'

Another photograph came out, a hand-tinted print of a young couple in wedding clothes, Walter Brown and his bride. Sheila looked at it for a few moments then set it down. The box was almost empty, apart from a few objects in the corners. She scooped them into one hand and put them on the desk, pushing them into a row, one by one.

There was a flat brass tab with a deeply stamped number on it. 'A lamp check,' she said. 'It belonged to Great-Grandad, the miner.' She turned it over to show the words 'North Wellwich Colliery Co.' stamped on the back. Next to it lay a pair of double-sided cufflinks, each face of chased silver and linked with fine chains.

'Grandpa's posh cufflinks,' she said. 'They were Great-Grandad's, too. He used to tell me how his mother gave them to her husband on their wedding day and they were the most valuable things he ever owned. Grandpa only ever wore them when he was being really flash.'

The rest were badges, a metal Labour Party badge, a CND lapel button, an Anti-Apartheid button, the broken rifle of the Peace Pledge Union, the stylised eye of the old National Council for Civil Liberties.

'What's that?' asked Sheila, separating one of the badges from the others.

It was a two-inch lapel button with a striking image of a skull in a gasmask and the word 'CHOKE!'.
'It's a local environmental group,' I explained. '"Community Health or Kerrenwood Enterprises". It was formed a few years ago to protest against a chemical disposal plant that they own here. They're one of those firms that import other countries' poisons and dispose of them "safely" here, usually by pouring them down old mineshafts so that they can seep into the water-table eventually.'

We both surveyed the display on the desktop for a while, then I said, 'Does any of it seem odd to you? Or is there anything missing?'

She shook her head. 'No,' she said. 'It's all there so far as I know, from an old miner's lamp check to this year's insurance receipts. The private museum of Walter Brown, deceased,' and she lifted her glass.

I drank with her, then topped up the glasses.

'So it doesn't help us?' I said.

'Not a bit,' she confirmed. 'So we'll have to try something else. Have you still got the house keys?'

'Yes,' I said, taking them from my pocket. 'You want to go back there?'

'No,' she said, and picked them up. 'Can I borrow your phone?'

I pushed the instrument across the desk and she looked at the key-tab before dialling. 'Since you refuse to sit at a long table and read the will to me and Mrs Croft, I shall have to meet her some other way.'

Her call was answered; she introduced herself to Mrs Croft and made an appointment to meet for afternoon tea at the Victoria.

'Shall I come along?' I asked as she replaced the phone.

'Not likely!' she said. 'I turn up with a lawyer and she'll think I'm going to accuse her of pinching the teaspoons and watering the washing-up liquid. No, we two girls both had an interest in Grandpa. Maybe she'll tell me what was biting him once we get cosy.'

She replaced the contents of the tin and slipped it into her capacious shoulder-bag. 'Tell John Parry, will you, that there wasn't anything he'd be interested in here,' she said. 'Then, if you're doing nothing tonight, I'll buy the tucker and you can tell me why you've been limping all day and never mentioned it. See you at the Victoria, seven thirty.'

7

There were fewer curious visitors to our table in the Jubilee Room that night. Instead, last night's people leaned across their tables and quietly told each other that Tyroll was over there, dining with that extraordinary Australian blonde.

Sheila watched the process and grinned. 'Are you some kind of superstar in Belston?' she asked.

'Far from it,' I said, ruefully. 'I told you – they think I'm some kind of subversive. Since you're an Aussie they probably think we're plotting the People's Republic of Belston. Anyway, Belston gossips out of habit. A barrister pal of mine says he loves doing cases up here because the gossip's better than in London.'

'Then you'd better come clean,' she said, 'before I have to get it off the gossips.'

'What do you mean?'

'I told you – if you fell over the cat last night you'd have said so, but you've been humping around like Long John Silver all day and not saying a word. Who did it to you?'

'I did it to myself,' I said, 'but if it'll satisfy your taste for the dramatic, I was escaping a drunken driver.'

Briefly I told her about the incident at my gate. I tried to play down any idea that it was deliberate, but I needn't have bothered. She became more serious as the story went on.

'Does this have anything to do with me – with Grandpa?' she asked.

'I doubt it,' I lied. 'If it was deliberate, and I'm not even sure of that, I've had attempts before. Some earnest lefties toughed me up last year for defending racists. The year before it was neo-Nazis having a go because I defended black men. One night I was crossing the square and a couple of guys were lolling about by the statue. As I passed by, one said, "Hey, man, what's in the briefcase?" I guess I was in line for a mugging, but the other said, "Lay off, man, that's my lawyer!" It's a tough old town, Sheila, and some of the people I deal with are some of its toughest.'

She smiled, but she also touched my hand across the table. 'Be careful, Chris,' she said. 'I'd never forgive myself if anything happened to you because of me.'

'Don't worry,' I said. 'I'm a card-carrying coward,' but her concern warmed me. 'Now then, what gossip did you drag out of Mrs Croft over tea and little cakes?'

'I'm not sure,' she said, 'but I think I might have a clue. Mrs Croft – who, incidentally, prefers port to tea by a long way – says that she "did for" my grandfather for four years. She was pretty cut up about his death, said she'd grown very fond of him while she worked for him. She said he was always very fair with her, and always remembered her kiddies' birthdays. When she'd done her stint for him each day they used to have a smoke together, what she called a "cuppa and bikkies" – '

'I know you're a social historian,' I interrupted, 'but is there much more before we get to the clue?'

She poked her tongue out at me, provoking wild speculation at those tables that noticed. 'I was just setting the scene,' she said, 'so you'd understand the context. Anyway, a few weeks ago he asked her if she knew any people called Cassidy in her area. Well, she prides herself on knowing everybody in town, apparently, but she didn't know any Cassidys.'

'Why'd he want to know?'

'She asked him that. He said he was trying to trace an old friend from years back, a Francis Cassidy that he knew during the war.'

'Did he ever mention Cassidy to you?'

'Not so as I remember,' she said, 'but I don't believe he ever did. Well, Mrs Croft was a bit piqued at not knowing Cassidy, so she asked about the neighbourhood and someone told her that there used to be Cassidys in North Belston until about the 1950s and they lived in Greenwell Lane.'

'It's been pulled down,' I said. 'They built the Orchard Estate on it in the sixties.'

She nodded. 'I know. She told me. She also told me that, eventually, someone told her there was an "old Cassidy" from the Greenwell Lane family still alive, but he was in an old people's home in Wellwich.'

'Did she know which one?'

'No, but a couple of days ago, when they were taking their smoke, he thanked her for finding out about Cassidy and said he was going to see him.'

'So your grandfather must have found out which one.'

'Right. Now is that a clue or not?'

I took a drink of wine and looked at her. 'What makes you think it's connected?' I asked.

'The letter,' she said. 'He wrote about "putting something right" and "wanting to see right done" before he died. That sounds like something that goes back a way. Then he starts looking for someone from years back. I'll tell you something else too. You know what an upright character my grandpa was?'

'Yes, indeed.'

'Well, Mrs Croft says that from all she's heard the Cassidys were famous villains – thieves, drunkards, what have you, always in and out of jail. I don't reckon old Cassidy sounds like any old mate of Grandpa's. He was looking for him for some other reason and he just said that to put Mrs Croft off the track.'

'Sounds like it,' I agreed. I took my diary out of my pocket and consulted it. 'I'm in court tomorrow morning, but you can spend the morning ringing all the old folks' homes you can trace in Wellwich and asking if Mr Cassidy is still there. When you've found him, we'll go and see him. Ask him what he and your grandad talked about.'

'So it is a clue?' she said.

'Indubitably, Watson,' I said. 'I reckon you deserve to share another bottle of wine with me as a mark of my regard.'

'Thanks for nothing,' she scowled. 'I happen to be paying.'

'It's the thought that counts,' I said, virtuously. 'Has anyone ever told you that you've got a very attractive scowl?'

When I reached the office next day, Jayne said, 'Your sun-raddled Aussie academic is in the waiting-room again,' and smirked.

'If', I said, 'you ever refer to that distinguished Antipodean lady in those terms again, I shall dismiss you forthwith. Any court in the world would accept my justification after one look at her. Where's the post?'

She passed me the post-folder. 'It's not the post you should be reading,' she said, 'but the "Guide to the Professional Conduct of Solicitors".'

'Thanks for the advice,' I said, 'but Dr McKenna is not a client. Have I opened a file for her? Have I opened a computer file? I am merely assisting a foreign lady in distress.'

'Well, aah,' she said, and went back to her word-processor.

Sheila was in good spirits. 'I've located him,' she said. 'He's at a place called Ferngate in Wolverhampton Road, Wellwich.'

'Did you make an appointment?' I asked.

'No,' she said. 'I wasn't sure how you were fixed.'

I flipped open my desk diary. 'I'm free this afternoon. Let's go!'

Twenty minutes later a cab dropped us outside Ferngate. It was a large, late-Victorian building with a wide, gravelled forecourt flanked by beech trees. We stood in the porch and I pulled the old-fashioned iron bell-pull. Somewhere inside there was a distant ringing.

Eventually the door swung open to reveal a harassed-looking teenager in a nylon overall. 'Can I help you?' she enquired.

'We'd like to see the person in charge,' I said.

'That'll be Miss Cromwell,' said the girl. 'Follow me, please.'

She led us through a tiled and panelled corridor to the back of the big house, and out on to a glass-roofed verandah that stretched the length of the building. It was dotted with chairs, tables and loungers.

'Miss Cromwell will be supervising luncheon at the moment,' said our guide, 'but if you'll take a seat I'll tell her you're here. What name was it?'

'Tyroll,' I said. 'I'm a solicitor.'

We chose seats and the girl left. I sniffed the air while Sheila looked around.

'A bit baronial, this,' she remarked. 'Is this on the National Health?'

'I should doubt it,' I said. 'Private care for the elderly is a booming racket in this country. You buy a big old place like this dirt cheap because there's very few sensible uses for it, hire a not very well qualified nurse to supervise and a couple of teenagers to do the work and sit back and count the money.'

'What are you sniffing for?'

'Analysis,' I said. 'Institutions all have characteristic smells. Schools smell of floor polish, paint and sweaty gym shoes, hospitals smell of ether, antiseptic and floor polish, prisons smell of boiled spuds, floor polish and sweaty people.'

'And what does this smell of?'

'Pee and lilac floor polish and loneliness.'

A lean, middle-aged woman appeared at the door and made for us. She wore a severely cut dark blue uniform with white plastic collar and cuffs.

'Mr Tyroll?' she said as she reached us, and stared from one to another of us as though Sheila might have been me.

I rose stiffly on my injured leg. 'Miss Cromwell,' I said. 'I'm sorry to call unannounced, but Dr McKenna here is from Australia and hasn't much time. I understand that a Mr Cassidy is an inmate here?'

'That is no longer true, Mr Tyroll. May I ask your business with him?'

I was taken aback by her answer but I tried to conceal it. 'We were told this morning that he was here,' I said.

'That will have been a mistake by one of my staff,' said Miss Cromwell, unruffled. 'Is this a legal matter?'

'No, no.' I said. 'Not strictly. Dr McKenna is the granddaughter of an old client of mine, a Mr Walter Brown. We understood that Mr Brown and Mr Cassidy were friends and that they might recently have met. You see, Dr McKenna's grandfather died the day before yesterday, and we wished to talk to Mr Cassidy as possibly the last person who had any conversation with him.'

'What an extraordinary coincidence!' exclaimed the supervisor. 'They did meet. Mr Brown visited Mr Cassidy here on Tuesday afternoon. They had a long chat out here, but I'm afraid you can't talk to Mr Cassidy. When Susan went to bring him in for his tea she thought he'd fallen asleep, but in fact he had passed away.'

'Passed away!' I echoed. 'Was Mr Brown still here?'

'Oh no. He'd gone about an hour before. So they both went on the same day. And their last meeting was here. How very curious and quite touching really.'

'Yes, indeed,' said I, while silently disbelieving that Miss Cromwell could be touched. 'Well, in that case I'm doubly sorry to have bothered you. Good afternoon, Miss Cromwell. Thank you for your time.'

47

We walked down the street to a callbox and rang for a cab. While we waited for it, we sat on a seat by a little green. I lit a cigarette. Sheila kept starting questions then stopping them in midstream.

When I had finished my cigarette I said, 'You're a historian, right?'

'Right,' she agreed.

'Do you believe in coincidence?'

'Not for a moment,' she said.

'Nor do I,' I said. 'Your grandfather certainly wasn't here the day before yesterday, but someone who used his name was. Someone who knew that Ferngate was expecting a visitor called Brown for Mr Cassidy, and knew that Walter Brown wasn't coming. Then Cassidy dies just after that interview. I'll bet you twenty quid to an Aussie dollar that your clue has just led us to another murder.'

8

I phoned John Parry from the callbox, telling him only that I had new and important information. When we arrived at the Rendezvous he was waiting for us at one of the back tables.

Ruby, seeing a customer of her own sex, bustled over to wipe the table and take our orders. When she'd gone Parry said, 'The whole division's running round in circles because of Lord Kerrenwood's visit, I'm trying to run a murder enquiry and you want to take tea. I hope you're going to make it worth my while.'

'Well, for starters I'm buying the teas,' I said.

'Must be important, then. Have you found anything in Mr Brown's tin box? Or something missing from it?'

'No,' said Sheila, 'but we've found something else. We think – '

I cut her short. 'We think we've a clue to what Sheila's grandfather was worrying about. Have you ever heard of a

48

family of villains who used to live in the Greenwell Lane area, before the estate was built there?'

'Have a heart,' said Parry. 'I'm not that bloody old! The Orchard Estate was built more than thirty years ago. Anyway, they were all villains, before and after the estate was built. Still are, most of them. You haven't, I suppose, got a name?'

'Does Cassidy ring any bells, sergeant?' asked Sheila.

'Cassidy, Cassidy,' he mused, gazing past us while he raked his memory. 'There's something very faint at the back of my mind. 1950s you say?'

I nodded. Ruby ambled down the aisle with the tea and Chelsea buns. The big Welshman was still gazing into the distance.

'Three teas, six buttered Chelseas. Who's paying?' Ruby demanded.

'He is,' said Parry, pointing at me, then, as I laid the money on the table, 'Ruby, you've seen every Belston villain for yonks. Do you recall a Cassidy family?'

'Course I do,' she said. 'The Cassidys was famous in their day. There was three brothers and they was all crooked, but the oldest was the worst, Francis. He'd steal anything. When I was in me teens he was in and out of here week in and week out, then he'd disappear for a bit when he got locked up, but it never stopped him. He never stopped till he won that money.'

'What was that?' I asked.

'Well, when he wasn't thieving or boozing or in jail he was betting. Course it wasn't legal then, all street-corner stuff. He came up on the pools in the end. He won thousands.'

'And what did he do with it?' asked Sheila.

'That's the funny bit, really. Everyone reckoned he'd have it up the wall in a week, but he didn't. He bought a house. Posh area west of Wolves. Never seen him since.'

She polished the table again with the corner of her apron. 'Blood will out, though, I always says,' she remarked.

'How do you mean?' said Parry.

'Well, you two ought to know, you and Mr Tyroll here. You been nicking his family for years and Mr Tyroll's been getting them off.'

We both stared at her. 'I can't recall a Cassidy,' I said and John Parry shook his head.

'Well, you wouldn't,' Ruby said, smugly. 'He had all daughters, you see. Four of them. That's the Waltons, the Kennedys, the Beales and the Parsonses. Don't tell me you don't know them!'

Parry and I both laughed ruefully at the too familiar names. 'So what happened to the old man?' he asked.

'Oh, he'll be dead now, or very old,' she said. 'Someone said he was in a fancy old folks' home, but that was a few years ago,' and she wandered away to her counter.

'So what's he got to do with Walter Brown?' said Parry.

It was my turn to be smug. 'Walter Brown died about eight o'clock Thursday morning, right?'

'Right.'

'Well, he had an appointment to see Francis Cassidy at Ferngate – the old people's home in Wellwich – that afternoon and someone called Brown kept that appointment.'

Parry's face was expressionless. 'Go on,' he said.

'About an hour after Brown left, they found Cassidy dead on the verandah.'

Parry continued to stare silently for a long time, then he shook his head slowly.

'Oh no,' he said. 'I won't buy that. You're not saying that someone did a Bulgarian umbrella job on him on the verandah at Ferngate. I am not having it.'

'You've got it, I'm afraid. It probably wasn't a poisoned umbrella, but if you get Macintyre to poke about in Cassidy's remains he'll find a murder for you.'

Parry leaned back from the table. 'But what was Brown going to see him about? Those two must have been like chalk and cheese. They can't have had anything in common, Chris!'

'They must have done,' said Sheila, 'or someone wouldn't have murdered them both on the same day.'

Parry stood up. 'Do you know how many murders we have in Britain?' he asked Sheila. 'About one a day for the whole damned country. England has the lowest murder-rate in the

Western world, envy of all we are, and you and Mr Tyroll here have just doubled the rate on my patch in one day.'

He turned away, then back again. 'If you should be right,' he said, 'that would mean that this thing is turning very sticky indeed. You'd be well advised to leave it alone now, both of you.'

Sheila looked genuinely innocent and I tried to. 'I', I said, 'will simply carry on trying to clarify instructions which a deceased client failed to specify properly.'

'And I', said Sheila, 'will carry on trying to find out what my grandfather knew that got him murdered.'

John Parry shook his head and hurried out of the Rendezvous.

Back at my desk, I got busy on the computer terminal.

'What are you doing?' Sheila asked.

'Calling up our file listings for Walton, Beale, Kennedy and Parsons,' I said. 'Ruby's right. We've had masses of them as clients. There's a juvenile Kennedy here with nineteen separate files.'

'How will that help us?' she asked.

'It'll give us addresses and phone numbers for this generation of the family, at least. With any luck we should be able to locate some older family who just might have an idea of what your grandfather had in common with Francis Cassidy.'

Soon I had a scribbled list of addresses and phone numbers. Taking the phone I began a series of calls. It was the fifth call before I jotted another note and put the instrument down with a grin.

'Got it!' I exclaimed. 'Granny Cassidy – Francis's widow – is still alive and I've got her address.'

'What are you going to do?'

'We are going to call on the lady this evening.'

'Her husband's just died. Do you think it's the right time?'

'I don't like to be heartless, but it may be just the right time. She may be in the mood for remembering old times.'

She was. When we arrived at the address I had been given, Mrs Cassidy, a small, bright-eyed lady, was obviously pleased to see us, driving away a couple of sympathetic neighbours and ushering Sheila and me into her front sitting-room. While she made tea we surveyed our surroundings.

The house was a three-bedroom semi, standing in a tree-lined street in Wellwich, and the room in which we sat was comfortably furnished with quality items. There were photographs on several surfaces and I recognised some smiling juveniles that I had seen with less affable expressions. I was still examining them when our hostess returned with a tray of tea and biscuits.

'That's my grandson, Wayne Beale,' she said, setting the tray down. 'You've had him through your hands, Mr Tyroll, haven't you?'

I nodded. 'How's he doing?' I asked.

'Got a job now,' she said, proudly. 'He's working for Kerrenwood's, like his grandad used to.'

'Your husband used to?' asked I, picking up the cue. 'If it wouldn't distress you, it's about your husband we came to talk. You see, Sheila here – Dr McKenna – has come over from Australia to visit her grandfather, but he had died before she got here. You may have seen it in the papers, he was attacked and killed in the park.'

The old lady nodded over her teacup. 'Wicked,' she said, 'bloody wicked that kind of thing is. My family ay saints, Mr Tyroll, as nobody knows better than you, but they don't go about hitting old men. Nor did my old man for all his faults. That was a wicked thing to do,' and she smiled sympathetically at Sheila.

'The thing is,' said Sheila, 'we believe my grandpa and the late Mr Cassidy knew each other. They had a meeting just before your husband died and I wondered what it was about. That's if it doesn't bother you to talk about it,' she added.

Mrs Cassidy smiled. 'It won't upset me, love,' she said. 'Francis and me was finished long ago. Divorced in '53, we were. It would've been a sight earlier than that if I'd had my way, but you had to catch 'em at it in them days, didn't you, Mr Tyroll?'

I wasn't even under articles when the old divorce law was changed, but I nodded, and the old lady went on.

'Francis knew lots of people,' she said. 'What was his name, your grandpa?'

'Brown,' said Sheila. 'Walter Brown. He used to work in the Town Hall before he retired.'

'Oh, I remember him!' exclaimed Mrs Cassidy. 'Big Labour Party man, wasn't he? He was really helpful to me about a council house for our June. She wouldn't have had it but for him.'

She shook her head slowly and went on. 'But I don't think he knew Francy at all. Me and him was separated by the time June wanted that house and June and me had to do it all. I don't think Francy ever met with Mr Brown at all.'

9

Sheila and I stared at each other, blankly. The old lady intercepted the look and leaned over, placing a small, wrinkled hand on Sheila's knee.

'Oh no, love,' she said. 'Your grandpa, Mr Brown, he was a gentleman, through and through. It was me that saw him about a house for June, not Francy. And Francy wouldn't have known him any other way. My Francy was so bent he couldn't lie straight in his bed and all his pals was the same. He wouldn't have gone near your grandpa, love, and your grandpa wouldn't have touched Francy with a bargepole.'

She sat back and it was Sheila's turn to shake her head. 'I don't get it,' she said. 'My grandfather wrote to me that he was trying to set something to rights before he died. It seems it was something that went back a long way. He told his cleaning lady that he was looking for an old mate – that was your husband – and he had a meeting with him at the home, Ferngate, the day that Mr Cassidy died.'

'And you thought it was about the same thing?' said Mrs

Cassidy. 'I don't blame you, duck. But I can't imagine what it could have been. Them two would have been like oil and water.'

I had been casting about in my mind for a solution to this new contradiction. I could not find one, but I was still convinced that Walter Brown's appointment with Francy Cassidy was central to the mystery. Why else had somebody impersonated the old man and why else had Francy Cassidy died? Mrs Cassidy seemed to have nothing useful to tell us, but I was unwilling to leave till we'd tried all the angles. I looked again at the framed snapshots dotted about the room.

'Mrs Cassidy,' I said, 'I don't think I ever met your husband. You haven't got a picture of him, have you?'

'No, Mr Tyroll, you wouldn't have done,' she agreed. 'You hadn't started up when Francy was in and out of the courts. He used to go to Mr Graham in Bull Street, but I can show you his picture. Just let me fresh the tea up.'

As the door closed behind the old lady, Sheila asked, 'Are you just fishing or have you got something in mind?'

'Trying to keep the conversation going,' I said. 'That appointment with Cassidy had to have been important and Mrs C's our only chance at the moment. But we don't know if she knows what we want to know, we don't know what it is so we can't ask her directly, and she may not even know that she knows.'

She smiled. 'Trust a Pommy lawyer to find a way of making the mysterious even more complicated.'

'That's why we charge so much – expertise! No, seriously, I may not have put that very well, but we've got to keep her talking about the late Francy and hope that something crops up that makes some kind of sense. And I was wondering if he's one of the men in the Victory picture.'

Mrs Cassidy was soon back with fresh tea and slices of fruit cake, which she urged on us. While we munched she got up and opened the cabinet on which her television stood, taking out a cardboard box. She brought it back and put it on the coffee table, beside the tea-tray.

'There,' she said, 'there's photographs here going back years.

I keep meaning to get one of the young ones to put them all in albums while I can still remember who they're all of, but all they want to do when they come round here is watch *Neighbours*.'

She dipped into the box and drew out a fistful of pictures of various sizes, including some in white presentation folders. Shuffling through them she separated one of the folders and opened it.

'There you are,' she said. 'That's me and Francy on our wedding day. 1939 that was, the summer before the war. Don't he look handsome?'

It was a black and white print that had been hand-tinted in peculiarly unnatural colours, and showed a bridal couple in front of a church door, surrounded by relatives. The bride was small and dark and strikingly pretty, while the groom was a tall, broad-shouldered young man, to whose pin-striped suit the colourist had applied a lurid shade of pinky brown.

'That's my Francy,' said our hostess. 'He looks good there, don't he? Course, he started putting on weight after we was wed. What with his drinking and never doing a hand's turn of work, he soon spread out.'

She poked among the other pictures and pulled out a small unmounted print. 'Look at that,' she said. 'That's just after the war, at Rhyl. One of those photographers on the promenade took it.'

This time it was just her and Francy. She was still trim and pretty in a bright print frock, but her husband's habits had thickened his waist and coarsened his features. A resemblance began to nag at the back of my mind.

'What did he do in the war?' asked Sheila. 'Was he in the forces?'

Mrs Cassidy laughed. 'Not him!' she said. 'Not my Francy. He didn't have to go, through bad feet. They were good enough at taking him to the pub, though, and when the air raid warnings went he was downstairs like a shot.'

'Did he have a civvy job?' I asked.

'Yes,' she said. 'He was a lorry-driver and there was always jobs for them in the war. Course, he was in and out of jail as well, because he couldn't keep his hands off his loads, but people was crying out for drivers and somehow he could usually find someone to set him on when he needed a job. And he was in the black market. What with everything being rationed or short, there was plenty of money to make on the black. Food, petrol, clothes, he used to flog them all. He must have made a lot of money one way and another, but what he didn't drink he gambled away. There was never enough to spare much for me and the kids, not even when he went straight, after the war.'

She shuffled through the photos again, silent with her reminiscences for a moment.

'That's him during the war,' she said, pulling out an eight by ten black and white print. Both Sheila and I were delighted to see that it was a larger version of the Victory group that had been in Walter Brown's tin box.

Mrs Cassidy passed it across and we examined it. Now we could see that one of the seated men was Francis Cassidy and in this version the man on the left, who had been incomplete in Walter Brown's copy, was shown in full, though neither of us recognised him.

'What's this picture of, Mrs Cassidy?' Sheila asked.

'I don't really know,' the old lady replied. 'You can see I wasn't there. He never took me boozing and that's him and his brothers and their boozing pals.'

'Is it one of the Victory days?' I asked. 'VE or VJ Day?'

She nodded. 'I expect that's right,' she said. 'They've all got their ration books, ay they? Oh, we thought rationing was all over then. Some folk were so daft they tore up their books on VJ Day. Then they was down the Food Office having to get new ones a day or two after. Some of them had to wait and they was fair desperate.'

'What did you do if you hadn't got a ration book?' asked Sheila, her historian's curiosity aroused.

'You went without, my duck. Or you paid for a black market book if you had the money. By the end of the war you could pay as much as eight or ten pounds for a dodgy ration book, so there wasn't many poor people saw them. It was only folks with a bob or two could afford them and they'd have second and third books to feed their faces with.'

'Did you say this was Francy and all his pals?' said I, trying to keep the conversation on course.

'Yes,' she said, 'they're all there. All his special mates.'

She took the photo back and pointed to each figure in turn. 'There's Francy,' she said, 'and that's his brother Bernard. He never went straight. He stayed a villain all his days and he died in Armley Prison in his sixties. That's the other brother, Martin. He was the youngest. He used to go mates with Francy when he had driving jobs. Even when they was bent ones.'

She chuckled inwardly at a recollection. 'Do you know how Francy paid for us wedding?' she asked. 'He had a driving job for a gang from Brum. With the factories getting ready for the war there was a lot of metal about and they'd heard that Bennetts had a big load of copper they could pinch. Well, they wanted a man as knew the back ways round Belston to drive the lorry, so they asked Francy. He wouldn't do it just for cash, he stuck out for a share and they give him one, but then it went wrong.'

'How was that?' asked I.

'Somebody must have talked in the wrong place, I don't know, but the police got to hear about it before they did it. Well, old Sergeant Reynolds, he come to Francy and questioned him about what he knew about it. Well, Francy wasn't going to cross up the Brummies, they had a name for being a bit handy with a razor in them days. He just told the sergeant as he day know anything about it. "You be sure you don't," says Reynolds, "'cos I shall be watching you."'

She chuckled again. 'And he was,' she said. 'He put a man on our street day and night. Poor old Francy couldn't go and put a bet on with Bert at the corner without the copper writing it down in his little black book. But they done it – they had that metal away from Bennetts' compound and Francy drove the lorry. Old Reynolds came round after, he was spitting blood. "We know you done it," he said to Francy. Francy just said, "If yo knows I done it, I daresay yo'll be able to prove it then," and old Reynolds he went bright red and stormed off.'

She paused and looked at the wedding photograph. 'We went to Blackpool after the wedding,' she said, 'and it was there Francy told me how he had paid the wedding bills and why we was having a late honeymoon. Well, I used to try not to encourage his thieving and that, but I couldn't help laughing at the way they did it.'

'How did they do it?' I asked.

'Francy sat upstairs, at the front window, every night, with the gas off, watching the copper across the street. Course, he was a plainclothes bobby and every night, after the first couple of nights, he'd pop round the corner about nine o'clock and settle in the snug at the Engineers Arms. Well, once Francy was sure of his man, he told the Brummies to come round with their lorry at the back just at nine one night. Soon as the copper went for his pint, Francy was out the back, into the lorry, and they had the job done and Francy back home before the pub shut. That was what made old Reynolds so mad – he knew how they'd done it, but he couldn't put his hands on Francy without having the story come out.'

She looked again at the wedding picture, and there was a trace of softness in her smile when she said, 'And that's how he paid the wedding bills and our honeymoon. Now he's gone and Sergeant Reynolds has had the last laugh.'

'How do you mean?' said I.

'How do I mean? Well, old Reynolds is still about, isn't he? He lives in Lime Avenue, with his daughter-in-law. He must be nearly a hundred years old by now.'

This time Sheila tried to steer the conversation. 'You were telling us about the blokes in the Victory photo,' she said.

'So I was.' The little hands picked up the picture again. 'There's Francy and Bernard and Martin, like I said. On the left there is Norman Berry, see how sharp he's dressed. He was all black market, he was. He made pots of money on the black. I calls him Lord Muckamuck, 'cos he always tried to make out he was better than everyone else. Still, he put Francy into a job at Kerrenwood's and it was the making of him in one way. He give up the drinking and gambling, and he had money – good money. But then he started after women. He wasn't half the man he'd been when we wed, but he had the money to pull them then and I got sick of it. So we split up, and he bought me out, as you might say. He got me this house and made an allowance for the girls and that was it.'

She ran a finger over the picture again. 'There's George Watson,' she said. 'He was a bookie's runner since before he left school, then he started into thievery. That one at the back, that's Freddy Thompson. He had a shop, a grocer's shop, but there was more went under his counter than over. He moved away after the war, so did George. I don't know where they went, up north I heard. That one there, that's young Alan Thorpe. He wasn't such a bad sort, just wild and daft he was. He used to go along with Francy and them just for a laugh. He's gone, too. He was always one for the girls and they found him dead one morning, in the gulley behind the Belston Arms. He'd been stabbed. They reckoned someone's husband or boyfriend had laid for him when he came out and settled a score with him.'

She laid the picture down and I picked it up. 'Is Martin still alive?' I enquired.

'No,' she said, shaking her head. 'He bought a car when the war ended. For a bit he had some kind of chauffeur business, but he never seemed to work at it. Still, he always had money in his pocket and he moved out to Kerrenwood Village. But the car was his end. He went in the canal driving home one Christmas Eve when he'd had too much. But you can't grieve for them. They was a bad lot who never did anyone but themselves any good, except by accident.'

She fell silent and I signalled Sheila and stood up. 'We've taken up a lot of your time, Mrs Cassidy,' I said, 'and we're very grateful. There's just one thing. Do you think I could borrow this picture of the Victory party long enough to get it copied? You can have it back tomorrow.'

'Take it, chuck,' she said. 'I don't need no reminders of that lot. Wrong uns, every one. If it helps you, you take it.'

She got up and saw us to the door. 'I'm only sorry I wasn't

more help,' she said. 'But I think you're barking up the wrong tree. I don't reckon your grandpa could have had any doings with Francy and his lot.'

I had taken a liking to the warm, bright-eyed little woman and, as we walked away, I hoped her dismissals of her former husband had been genuine and would stand her in good stead when she was told that he had been murdered.

10

We sat in the Rendezvous, sipping tea and staring at the Victory photo. The two versions lay side by side on the table between us.

'Well,' said Sheila, 'you tell me, Chris. Does anything she said make any sense?'

'I really don't know,' I said. 'I'm not even sure I can remember all of it.'

'No problems, counsellor,' she said, brightly, and delved into her capacious shoulder-bag. After a quick rummage she pulled out a small black case and put it on the table. 'There you are,' she announced triumphantly. 'The wonders of microtechnology. All on tape.'

I shook my head. 'It's come to a pretty pass,' I declared, 'when little old ladies can't take tea with a passing historian without being covertly taped. What else have you got in that bag? A brace of six-shooters? A spy camera? Pair of handcuffs?'

'I'd heard you Poms were into kinky sex,' she said. 'Just drink your tea and try to keep calm. The old dilly bag is for emergencies – like when people get put off by notebooks and start acting when they can see your tape-recorder. You ought to be grateful.'

'Oh, I am, I am,' I assured her and called to Ruby for some scrap paper. She brought me a six-page letter from the local Health Department and another round of teas.

Together Sheila and I went through the tape, trying to

summarise what Mrs Cassidy had told us. After an hour and more tea we had two pages of notes on the back of Ruby's correspondence:

Francis Cassidy
Married Mrs C in summer 1939
Late honeymoon & wedding pd. for by share of Bennetts' loot – put it over Sgt Reynolds on Bennetts' job.

Wartime: straight & bent driving jobs
          in and out of jail
          black market, thieving, gambling
          young brother Martin as mate on some driving jobs
          At least one big job for a Brummy gang (Bennetts' copper)

Postwar: Holiday at Rhyl
          Steady job at Kerrenwood's (fixed by Norman Berry)
          Good money, womanising
          Divorced 1950s
          Bought Mrs C house in Wellwich, allowance for daughters

Victory piccy: Francy C
          brother Bernard (died in Armley nick)
          Young brother Martin, had some kind of chauffeur business but didn't really work at it – drowned in canal
          George Watson (bookie/thief)
          Freddy Thompson (bent grocer)
          Alan Thorpe ('wild' – womaniser)
          stabbed in gulley by B. Arms (when?)
          vengeful hubby/boyfriend?
          Norman Berry – sharp dresser, snob (Lord Muckamuck) moved to Kerrenwood
          Village – fixed Francy's job with Kerrenwood's

Sgt Reynolds: Pissed off by FC's trick in Bennetts' robbery
Still alive – Lime Avenue, Wellwich.

Sheila switched off the tape and put the little recorder away. I passed her the notes.

'Any ideas?' she asked, when she had scanned the papers for a couple of minutes.

'Not unless it's the vengeance of Sergeant Reynolds, no.'

'There's a couple of references to Kerrenwood's. That's where Mrs Cassidy said her grandson worked. What is it? Didn't she mention a Kerrenwood Village? Is it a place or a firm or what?'

'It's a firm,' I said. 'Kerrenwood Enterprises.'

'That's right,' she interrupted. 'There was a badge in Grandpa's tin. What did you say it was? CHOKE?'

'Community Health or Kerrenwood Enterprises,' I recited. 'They've got a huge plant out on the edge of town, between the town and Kerrenwood Village. They ship in chemical waste from all over – Britain and abroad – and reprocess it so it's supposed to be harmless, then they pour it down eighteenth-century mineshafts that have never been properly surveyed. CHOKE says that sooner or later it all seeps into the water-table and poisons us. They also do nuclear processing. They've got rubber-burning facilities and lots of chimneys pumping fumes across Belston.'

'Why aren't they stopped?'

'Who by? CHOKE is just concerned residents who don't want to be poisoned. There's not a single councillor in it. Kerrenwood's employ a lot of people and buy a lot of services. This town lost all its heavy industry in the early eighties. There are still tower blocks in the Meadows with eighty per cent unemployment. Nobody's going to shut Kerrenwood's down and wipe out all those jobs.'

She looked thoughtful. 'Do you think Grandpa went up against them?' she asked.

'Well, he kept his CHOKE button in his little box, so he certainly wasn't a fan of Kerrenwood's, but what are you saying? You think Kerrenwood Enterprises killed him – and Francy Cassidy?'

62

'Maybe he found out something about Kerrenwood's. Something he wanted to confirm with Cassidy. Something that might close them down or harm them. That'd cost someone a hell of a lot of money, wouldn't it?'

'Well, yes,' I agreed. 'Kerrenwood's is a privately owned company. None of this "share-owning democracy" rubbish there. It all belongs to Lord Kerrenwood and his clan. I suppose they'd have to take a considerable reduction in the champagne budget if any large part of Kerrenwood's went. But they don't have to kill people to protect themselves. They buy people. His Lordship's a huge conributor to the government, personal pal of the PM, grey eminence of the party for years. He doesn't need hitmen, he's got money and influence.'

'He reprocesses nuclear waste,' she said, doggedly. 'You said Grandpa's death smelt of – what did you call them? The funnies? What about your nuclear police? Mightn't they have got after Grandpa and Cassidy to shut something up?'

'I suppose they just might,' I said, but I didn't really believe it.

'Have you got any better ideas, then?' she demanded.

'I don't know if it's better, but there's something that strikes me as odd here. There's seven men in a pub in 1945 – '

'Eight,' she interrupted.

'Eight?'

'Eight,' she repeated. 'Somebody took the picture.'

'The landlord,' I said.

'The landlord? How do you know?'

'Because', I said, pointing to the larger picture, 'that blurred object down the left side is a beer-handle, so it was taken from behind the bar.'

'OK,' she surrendered. 'There were seven men and the landlord in a pub in 1945 – this is beginning to sound like the beginning of a joke.'

'You want my ideas, you listen to them,' I said, picking up the notes. 'Seven blokes, all mates, partners in crime. What's happened to them?' I tapped a finger down the sheet of notes.

'Francy Cassidy – lived to ripe old age, but got murdered;

Bernard Cassidy – lived to middle age and died in nick; Martin Cassidy – died in an accident, comparatively young; George Watson, Freddy Thompson – both left the area; Alan Thorpe – murdered comparatively young; Norman Berry – apparently made it good at Kerrenwood's.'

I looked at her, expectantly.

'What are you trying to say?'

'It's an awful lot to happen to a handful of ordinary blokes who survived the war without getting shot or bombed by Adolf Hitler.'

'But they weren't ordinary blokes,' she said. 'They were all dodgy coves, all crooks. Some of them were always heading for sticky ends and some of them met them.'

'I don't know,' I said. 'This list gives me a feeling that something particular was at work, something with money in it. Ruby says Cassidy won the pools, but his wife never mentioned it. She only said he had better money after he worked for Kerrenwood's.'

'Maybe Ruby's wrong.'

'Never known it,' I said. 'Somewhere there's a lot of money in this. More than they made as petty black marketeers, spivs, thieves – '

'What's a spiv?'

'If you're going to come to our country, Dr McKenna, you really should learn the language. "Spiv" – a term from the war, meaning a seller of dodgy goods, forged petrol coupons, what have you. From the old coppers' abbreviation "SP/IV" – "suspected person or itinerant vagabond".'

'Thank you, Professor Tyroll. Now, carry on about them being small-timers.'

'They seem to have ended up with a lot of money after the war. And too many of them got killed. Two separate murders and a fatal accident among seven blokes. I don't know what an actuary might make of it, but it smells fishy to me. That's a murder rate of nearly thirty per cent! We're supposed to have the lowest murder rate in the Western world.'

'That's if there really have been two murders. What if Cassidy simply pegged out from old age and boredom?'

'He didn't,' said a Scottish voice and there was Dr Mac beside the table, clutching a mug of tea.

He slid himself on to the bench alongside Sheila and picked up the photographs and notes, glancing at them and dropping them again.

'If', he said, 'you were discussing the late Francis Cassidy, you may accept my word for it – he was murdered.'

'How?' we both asked at once.

The pathologist took a long draught of tea. 'On your hypothesis, John Parry has deeply upset Messrs Ryland and Lloyd, Undertakers, by seizing a cadaver from their pretty wee chapel and having me work my wicked will on it. He has also deeply upset me, by requiring me to try and determine the cause of death of a corpse that had been shaved, waxed, painted and God knows what else. Nevertheless, science has triumphed. Francis Cassidy was suffocated.'

We waited for more while he reapplied himself to his mug.

'Once the make-up had been removed,' he said, 'it was evident that Cassidy was stifled. From the inside of the mouth I removed purple velvet fibres that came from a cushion at Ferngate.'

'Who do you think did it?' Sheila asked.

'I am by way of being one of the best of my unlovely and unpopular profession, lassie, but I am not psychic. If I was I would suggest that misfortune will come your way if you don't leave this affair to John Parry and the professionals.'

'Oh, come on, Doc,' she exclaimed. 'John Parry has got a boss who's running interference on someone's behalf, and you and I both believe there's a department of the government involved! What's going to happen if I leave it to the police? I'll tell you – my poor old grandfather will become just another bloody unsolved murder statistic! Well, I'm not going to have it!'

Her cheeks had flared. Now she pushed out of the bench seat, nearly throwing Macintyre into the aisle, and marched out.

There was a long, sticky silence, then 'Thanks, Doc,' I said.

'It's true, laddie,' said the old man. 'This case felt bad from the first. Now it smells bad, and you ought to know better than to let her get mixed up with it.'

'She is mixed up with it, Mac. Walter Brown was her only living relative.'

'Then put her on a plane tomorrow. Let her go back to Adelaide and remember her grandad the way she knew him as a wee girl. She'll do nae good here.'

I shook my head. 'It wouldn't work, Doc. If I try to persuade her to back off, she'll go it alone. I couldn't do that.'

Macintyre looked up at me sharply. 'No,' he said, after a moment. 'I don't suppose you could. Ah weel, we were all young and daft once.'

'If the Devil should cast his net . . .!' exclaimed a Welsh voice. 'Jayne said you were probably here. Where's our gracious Aussie doctor?'

'Weeping in her hotel room, I imagine,' said Macintyre, 'because, Sergeant Parry, she believes that you're not going to solve her grandad's murder.'

'I have come', said the detective, 'to tell you that your suspicions were correct, but I see I have been forestalled.'

'Any idea who did it?' asked I.

'Well, now, I suppose I shouldn't tell you, but I will since you put us on to it. The "Mr Brown" who called at the home was a tall athletic gent with a posh accent.'

'Did he, by any chance,' I asked, 'have an equally posh sports jacket with a missing button?'

'He certainly had a sports jacket,' said Parry, 'though nobody counted the buttons. He also had a blue saloon that waited for him on the forecourt. What about that?'

'It waited for him?' I repeated. 'You mean it had a driver? Let me guess – it had a driver who was dark and unshaven and wore a leather jacket, right?'

'Right,' confirmed Parry.

'Why are you telling me this?'

'So you can explain to the lady that you were right, that Her Majesty's funnies or someone very much like them killed Walter Brown and that she'd be well advised to forget it and go home to Lucky Oz.'

'She has been well advised,' I said, 'by our Scottish pal here. She stormed out of here after forcibly expressing the view that you would never solve the case because your boss wouldn't let you.'

I dropped a handful of coins on the table and stood up, picking up the photos and notes.

'You're buying grief, boy,' warned Parry, 'you're buying grief.'

'Sheila's got grief. She didn't buy it. Some bastard gave it to her.'

It was my turn to stride out of the Rendezvous.

11

I didn't follow Sheila to the hotel. I went back to the office and tried to do some work. It was useless. All I could think of was Sheila and her problems. A lot of my thinking was about the lady rather than the problems. It had been a good many years since a woman had appealed to me so strongly, and I cursed my ill-luck that it should be an Australian who was only going to be around for weeks at the most. At the same time, I could see the truth of the warnings from Parry and Doc. Whatever had brought about Walter Brown's death was complicated and secret. Maybe Sheila was right, perhaps it did have to do with Kerrenwood's nuclear involvement – I'd read all the rumours about the 'nuclear police' and their alleged use of deadly force.

Whatever my feelings towards Sheila, I knew that I ought to persuade her to go home. Someone had killed twice to protect something. They might have killed three times if I hadn't still been able to vault my own front gate. Nuclear police or not, someone was using deadly force, and I knew I'd never forgive myself if any harm came to her.

I sat at my desk while the office shut down for the day. Jayne and the other staff popped their heads round the door to say goodnight and I responded mechanically.

I would never persuade Sheila to go home. However much I wanted to, I'd seen enough of her feelings for her grandfather and enough of her tough, enquiring personality to know that she would never walk away while Walter Brown's death remained unresolved. What I had said to Macintyre and John Parry was true and that meant there was only one answer. I had to help her.

The next move? I recalled the men in the photograph. All dead or vanished except – except Norman Berry. I picked up the telephone directory. There were eleven Berrys listed. I rang each one, introducing myself and trying to suggest that there was an inheritance in the offing. Nobody took the bait. None of them had a relative called Norman.

I didn't know where to go next. We could not ask Parry for further assistance. It would place the sergeant in an impossible position. I thought for a moment, then picked up the phone again and punched out the number of Belston police station.

The police switchboard put me through to the duty desk and I was pleased to hear the familiar voice of Sergeant Crow.

'Duty desk. Sergeant Crow speaking. What can we do for you?'

'Good evening, sergeant. Chris Tyroll here.'

'Mr Tyroll! What can I do for you? We haven't got any of yours in tonight.'

'Good, I hope it stays that way. I was looking for some information, actually. Have you ever come across a retired sergeant called Reynolds?'

Crow laughed. 'Everybody on the force knows Reggie Reynolds. We call him our oldest living inhabitant. We've got a fund up in the bar. We all put into it and each one draws a month between now and Reggie's hundredth birthday. If he makes his century the money'll go to a big party for him. If he snuffs it before the big one hundred then the bloke with the right month wins the pool.'

'I wouldn't let that get about, if I were you, sergeant. If he drops off suddenly some suspicious copper might think the winner had fixed the result.'

Crow laughed again. 'Could be,' he said. 'Anyway, what's your interest in old Reggie?'

'I've been looking into some old Belston cases and someone thought Sergeant Reynolds might be able to help. How old is he?'

'Older than God's dog,' he said. 'Well, he's well past ninety, any road. He was a sergeant sixty-odd years ago. Standing joke round here when anyone puts their stripes up, we always tell them if they're not careful they'll end up wearing them as long as old Reggie.'

'Is he all right – I mean, is he still *compos mentis*?'

'Well, he was last time I saw him. We always have him up the bar on his birthday and give him a bit of a treat. Couple of months ago we had the force helicopter in and took him for a spin. Lapped it up, he did. Oh, he's sharp as a tack most of the time, just rambles a bit. If you listen long enough you'll hear about every crime committed in this town since the Great War.'

'He lives in Lime Avenue, I think?'

'That's right. I can't just recall the number, but it's a double-fronted house on the right as you go up from town. If you see him, give him my regards.'

'Thanks, sergeant.'

I flipped the receiver rest then punched in another number, for the Victoria. Sheila answered from her room. She sounded withdrawn, wary.

'I wondered', I said, carefully, 'if I might feed you again tonight?'

'Not if you're going to tell me to push off home like a good little girl,' she said. 'I don't need a meal that badly.'

'I think you've got me mixed up with a certain detective and a mad old Scotsman,' I said. 'I don't know if I'm smarter than them or a lot dafter, but whichever it is, I'm not going to tell you to go home.'

'On that understanding,' she said, 'I'll see you in the residents' bar about seven thirty.'

She looked tense and pale when we met. Normally she knew that she needed little make-up, but now she had made up her

69

eyes to conceal the redness at their rims. I said nothing until the food had been ordered.

'You've been crying again,' I said, softly.

'Yes, I have,' she said, shortly. 'And you say half a wrong word and I'll start again, right here. That'll give your posh Pommy pals something to gossip about!'

'You had to cry for your grandfather,' I said.

'I wasn't crying for him. I've done that. I was bloody crying for me. Some ratbag chopped my grandpa down and rolled him under a bush like junkies rolling an old tramp. Walter Brown was worth better than that and I want those bastards nailed – I don't care if they're Her Majesty's funnies, the nuclear police or the Prime Minister's nephews, I want them locked up for every second the law allows, and all anyone'll tell me is "Give it up and go home."'

She was close to tears again. I reached across and clasped my hand around hers on the stem of her glass.

'I'm not saying that,' I said. 'I agree with you – whoever it was should suffer for it, but what Parry and Doc said was true. It's extremely dangerous, but you know that. I just wanted to say that I'll help you any way I can, but you'll have to forgive me if I spend some time now and then worrying about you getting hurt.'

She rolled her hand in mine and clenched my fingers fiercely. 'Strewth!' she said. 'A real, old-fashioned Pommy gent!'

'All solicitors', I said, solemnly, 'are gentlemen. That's why so many crooks join the game. It gives them status without responsibility. Now – can we talk about who wrote "Waltzing Matilda" or why Australians talk funny?'

So we did, and four hours later, when I took a cab from outside the Victoria, I knew that if there'd ever been any doubt I was now certain: there was nothing on earth I less wanted Sheila McKenna to do than go back to Australia – ever.

I usually stay awake into the early hours – sometimes I'm working till three – but that night I fell asleep quickly. The phone shattered my romantic dreams at three o'clock in the morning. It was John Parry.

'You'd better get down here, Chris! Your office is on fire. We think it's arson.'

When a cab dropped me in the square I saw John Parry, standing with his superintendent alongside the fire engine. The night was close and warm and the thick, dark smoke that was still pouring out of the entry to the building was spreading across the square like a dark ground fog, drifting around the engine and the feet of the small crowd that, despite the hour, were being urged back by a couple of uniformed policemen. The blue and red strobe lights from the fire appliance and the police cars, flickering on the drifting smoke, and the throbbing of pumps and generators made the whole thing look and sound unreal, more like a clip from *Top of the Pops* than an urban fire scene.

Superintendent Howard saw me alight from the cab and strode across, setting his jaw in advance to deal with someone he intensely disliked.

'Mr Tyroll.' He nodded sharply. 'Your premises are on the first and second floors, aren't they?'

'Yes,' I confirmed. 'What's happened?'

'The first-floor rear area of the building has been set alight, apparently by arson.'

'Arson!' I repeated. 'Sergeant Parry said that on the phone. Why do you think it's arson?'

'There was a courting couple in the yard at the back. They phoned us and the brigade. They say they saw someone in the yard who flung something through the first-floor back window and then threw something else after it that burst into flames.'

I shook my head. 'Did they give a description of the – the arsonist?'

Howard hesitated. 'No,' he said. 'The courtyard was very dark.'

'Did they see a car?' I persisted. 'A dark blue saloon perhaps?'

'You have some idea who did this?' asked Howard, without answering my question.

'If it was arson I can only think of one explanation.'

71

'I imagine it may have something to do with some of your more political clients,' said Howard.

'No. Not this time. Hasn't Sergeant Parry spoken to you about the Walter Brown murder?'

'The Brown case?' Howard's protuberant eyes widened. 'That's merely a mugging. What could this have to do with that?'

'Brown's death seems to have to do with the murder of old Francy Cassidy,' I said. 'Why shouldn't it be connected with arson?'

'I don't know what you're talking about,' snapped Howard. 'In any case, I can't discuss police enquiries with you. You'd better tell John Parry what you know about this matter,' he said, dismissively, and strode away to his car.

I walked across to Parry. 'What's he doing up and about at this time of night?' I asked, jerking a thumb towards the superintendent's departing car. 'It's bad enough being fire-bombed without him lying to me at three o'clock in the morning.'

'He told me', said Parry, evenly, 'that he just happened to be in the control room when the call came in. Lying to you, was he?'

'Of course he was. You've got a description, haven't you? Tell me, was it the bloke in the leather jacket or his boss with the posh sports coat?'

Parry's features did not change; nor did he reply.

After a long moment I walked off and joined the fire brigade chief.

I introduced myself and asked, 'Is there much damage?'

'Not as much as there might have been if those kids hadn't called us,' said the chief. 'The first-floor back room is in a mess. My blokes are just making it safe.'

'Can I see?' I asked.

'Not now,' said the chief. 'Better leave it till morning. We'll make it secure till then, but we're not sure the floor's safe.' He called Parry across. 'John! Show Mr Tyroll what we found.'

Parry came across, carrying a blackened brick. He held it under one of the engine's lamps so that I could see it. Underneath the smoke blackening two words were still visible in white paint – 'TROTSKYITE BASTARD'.

I straightened up from examining the brick. 'I suppose that's supposed to mean that someone like the England First mob did it? That's what Superintendent Howard thinks – or what he wants me to think.'

Parry smiled enigmatically.

'If that's what Superintendent Howard thinks, it must be true, isn't it?'

12

Having a fire is like being drunk. Through the confusion you occasionally realise that it's going to be a lot worse in the morning and it usually is. To my surprise, when I came to examine my premises next day, the damage was not so bad as I had feared.

The first-floor rear room is a small filing area, its walls ranked with steel filing cabinets and fire-proof cupboards in which we keep wills, property deeds and other documents that require especial safety. I had had visions of a heap of melted metal and ash representing the proof of the worldly wealth and intentions of many of my clients, but walking through the room with the fire officer and John Parry in the morning I was relieved to see that the cabinets had held.

The fire officer showed us an area under the broken window which had evidently been the seat of the fire. From just beneath the window an ellipse spread into the room, across which the floorboards had burned through to the joists.

'After the brick to break the window,' said the fireman, 'they flung an incendiary device of some kind. There were pieces of a bottle and you can smell the spirit. It was probably just a petrol-bomb.' He pointed to a heap of ash alongside the ellipse. 'What was that?'

I stooped and picked up some of the crumbling flakes. 'They

must have been documents,' I said, 'but they weren't here before.'

Turning to the nearest cupboard I tried the handle. It was jammed. I pulled out the top drawer of an adjacent filing cabinet. It was empty.

'That's what it was,' I said. 'The files out of this cabinet.'

Quickly I pulled out the three lower drawers. They were still full. 'It wasn't just an arson attack,' I said. 'Someone must have been in here first, selected the cabinet, emptied the top drawer and then gone off and staged an arson attack to burn the files.'

'What were they?' asked Parry.

'Letters A to E, including, of course, the files for Walter Brown. They looked for something in his files and wouldn't have found anything. Just in case they'd missed something, they tried to burn the place and destroy whatever it might have been. Anyway, I'd better stop messing with things. No doubt your Scenes of Crime man will be wanting to look for fingerprints.'

'Shouldn't worry about that,' said Parry, as straight-faced as he had been the night before. 'Superintendent Howard has already told me to pull in the loonies from England First and sweat them.'

'Basing his conclusions, no doubt, on the fortuitous evidence of the brick,' I said, sarcastically.

'No doubt,' agreed the sergeant. 'It is frequently remarked in the tabloid papers that it is only the stupidity of criminals that allows us poor plods to catch them, and it is a fact well known in police circles that arsonists frequently leave behind a piece of specially prepared, non-inflammable evidence that will clearly point to them as the perpetrators. Famous for it, they are.'

The fire chief was bemused by the unspoken tension between me and Parry. 'Unless there's anything else either of you wants, I'll be going,' he said.

When he had gone we moved to my office and I called Jayne in.

'It looks like we've lost only one drawerful of old files and a big piece of floor,' I said. 'Get someone in to fix that floor, will you, and check the fireproof cabinets. I tried the handle on one and it's jammed. Oh, and get Sandy to bring us some coffee, please.'

When she'd gone I looked at the big Welshman. 'Well,' I said, 'I suppose you want a statement now?'

Parry shook his head. 'Not at all,' he said. 'We've got the evidence of the courting couple last night and we know what damage was done. You weren't here. You can't help. Instructions from above are to roust out all the known England Firsters and sweat them. What'll you do if we end up charging one of your old clients?'

'Defend him, probably. At least I'll have the rare advantage of being certain he's innocent.'

We were drinking our coffee in silence when the door opened and Sheila walked in unannounced.

'I might have known I'd find you here,' she remarked to Parry.

He stood up. 'Just taking a brief break from the endless struggle against the powers of darkness, Dr McKenna,' he said, 'but the battle cannot wait. Good-day to you,' and he left.

As soon as he was gone Sheila dropped into the chair he had vacated. 'Are you all right, Chris? I heard about the fire on the local radio news. They said it was a bomb.'

'I'm fine,' I said. 'I was fast asleep at home when it happened. However, I can't say I like sitting in an office that reeks of burned timber, wondering who burgled my files and threw a firebomb.'

'They burgled you as well?'

Quicky I explained to her that the fire had been caused to cover up the theft or destruction of her grandfather's files.

'But you said there was nothing much in them.'

'There wasn't. The only items that mattered were the deeds of his house and the original of his will. They were in the fireproof cabinets and, so far as we know, they've survived.'

'Then what were they after?'

'If they stole his files it was because they thought there was something in them that mattered. If we knew what it was, then we'd know what this is all about and probably who killed him

75

– which brings me to my next point. Which is that when they read the stolen files they will realise there isn't anything in them. So they'll try again.'

'They'll try what?'

'They'll decide, perhaps, that if I haven't got the McGuffin then I must have given it to you. Then they'll come after you.'

If I had intended that argument to make her think, I was disappointed.

'What's a McGuffin?' she asked, brightly.

'It's what Alfred Hitchcock called the thing that everyone's looking for in a thriller. But, don't you see? You're about to become a target.'

'Now hold on,' she said. 'Don't start with that "Why don't you go home?" stuff.'

'I wasn't. I told you last night I wouldn't. But we're trying to do two things at once. We're trying to work out what's happening and who's doing it and we're also having to deal with the things they are doing, like burgling houses and offices, trying to run people over – killing people, Sheila.'

'So what do you suggest? We send a bloke out with a white flag and call a cease-fire?'

'No. I suggest that you vanish. What's more, I suggest that I vanish with you. That will do two things, it'll throw them off balance and it'll give us some time to try and think it out.'

'Where are we going to vanish to?'

I pulled out a drawer of my desk and poked around inside it, eventually coming up with business card. It was large, black, shiny and embossed with several lines of Old English type in silver. I passed it to her.

'That's a bed and breakfast place in North Bromwich. Pack up at the Victoria, pay your bill and make sure they know you're going to London on business connected with your grandfather's death. Then take a cab to the station and catch a train to North Bromwich, it's only two stops. You'll be OK there.'

'What is it?' she said, looking at the ornate card.

'Mrs Breadwell runs a superior boarding-house. I once did

her son a great favour, or so she thinks, so when people are looking for one of my clients in Belston, I send them to Mrs B, who looks after them and keeps her trap shut.'

'You're all romance, you Pommies. You promise to take me away from all this and it turns out to be a boarding-house in North Bromwich!'

'Ingrate,' I said. 'This is a temporary measure. Tomorrow we have another potential witness to interview, after that I shall lure you away to my country retreat for a little while.'

She tucked the card in her bag and stood up. 'Don't forget to ring me once you're safe in the motherly bosom of Mrs Breadwell,' I said and reached for my desk diary and the phone.

'Jayne,' I said, 'don't wait for the next office meeting. Get me a mobile phone today – a good one. And is anyone using the Shanty this weekend? They're not? Good, can I borrow it? Thanks. Oh, and ask Alasdair to cover Monday's cases.'

When Sheila phoned two hours later to report that she was installed in North Bromwich I felt a weight lift from my mind. We met that evening in a Spanish restaurant in North Bromwich where the proprietors know that paella can be made with lamb instead of frozen prawns. We were at the coffee stage when I noticed a young woman standing at the bar. She was a slight, pretty blonde, overdressed and over-made-up. With a start I recognised one of my clients, a teenage prostitute from Belston's notorious 'Relief Road'.

She saw me looking at her and made a beeline for our table.

'No, it's all right, Mr Tyroll,' she said as I pulled out a chair for her. 'I can't stop. I just came with a message. Warren's outside and he needs to talk to you – urgent. But he doesn't want to be seen.'

I looked around and caught the manager's eye, bringing him hurrying across.

'Everything all right, Mr Tyroll?' the tall Spaniard asked.

'Everything's fine, Lario, but I need to talk to someone in private. Can you do anything?'

'No problem, Mr Tyroll. You can have the private room. Nobody's in there. Follow me.'

77

He led us quickly into a small but luxuriously furnished dining-room with a six-seater table.

'Tracey,' I said, 'go out and bring Warren in the back way, through the kitchens. Lario will show you how to bring him through. Lario, can we have another round of coffees, for four this time?'

In seconds the girl was back, accompanied by a stocky man in his thirties. He wore an expensive leather jacket over a T-shirt printed with a Union Jack. His hair was cropped almost to the skull and his face and hands were tattooed. He smiled broadly at Sheila and me and sat down. The girl excused herself and slipped out.

'Sheila,' I said, 'this is Warren Saxon, Regional Secretary of the England First Party. Warren, meet Dr Sheila McKenna of Adelaide.'

Warren nodded affably. 'Pleased to meet you, miss,' he said. 'I'm sorry about your grandfather,' and he sounded as if he meant it.

Lario brought the coffees in and they stayed silent till he was gone. Then Sheila said, 'What exactly does your party believe in, Mr Saxon?'

'An Anglo-Saxon England,' he said promptly, putting four spoonfuls of brown sugar in his coffee. 'Nationalisation of the banks and insurance companies, repatriation of immigrants – '

'Cut the politics, Warren,' I said. 'If you know that Dr McKenna is Walter Brown's granddaughter you must have been doing your homework.'

'Oh, I have, Mr Tyroll, I have. Because I've been having some homework done on me. No doubt the filth have told you that my boys did your office last night?'

I nodded.

'Well, we didn't. We ain't ungrateful, you know that. We come to you when we got trouble and you do your best. We ain't gonna bomb your gaff, are we?'

'I never thought you did,' I said, 'but is that all that this is about?'

'Oh, no. This is about who did do it, Mr Tyroll.'

'Do you know?' I asked, sharply.

'I know who offered us a – er, contribution to party funds if we'd do it.'

'And who was that?'

'A bloke I've never even seen before, let alone done business with. He never gave me a name, but he was English, expensive education I reckon, dressed expensive too. Sounded and looked like an ex-Special Services officer to me.'

'And what exactly did he want you to do?'

'He wanted us to go into your office, snatch all the files on a certain old gentleman and then burn the place. We turned it down. We got loyalties, you know, you're nothing if you ain't got loyalties. But that is what happened last night, isn't it, Mr Tyroll?'

I nodded. 'Plus the fact that the window was broken with a brick with "TROTSKYITE BASTARD!" painted on it, pointing the finger at you and your pals,' I said.

Warren shook his cropped head disapprovingly. 'They never get their politics right, do they, the funnies? I know you ain't a Trotskyite. If I'd have done it that brick would have said "BLOODY ANARCHIST!"'

We all chuckled, then I asked, 'Is that who you think he was, the man that offered you? DI5 or 6 or 9?'

'Something like that,' said Warren. 'But I wouldn't like to guess exactly what. But that's not the important bit. The reason I came was that he's been back to me, tonight.'

I stared at him.

'Oh, yes,' he said. 'He's made me another offer. He'll get the filth off my boys' backs if we'll do a job for him, and he'll bung us.'

'And what is it this time?'

Without looking up from his coffee, Warren said quietly, 'He wants the lady, here. He wants Dr McKenna.'

13

Sheila and I stared at him, as our suspicion became fact.

I broke the silence. 'What did you tell them?'

'I told him I'd see what I could do. I had to, Mr Tyroll. He'd made things very difficult for me with that firebombing.'

'And now you've tracked us here, what are you going to tell him?' I asked, grimly.

'I'm going to tell him as the staff at the Victoria say that the lady's gone to London and she hasn't kept her booking,' said Warren. 'There's not much I can do for him in the Smoke that he can't do better and that'll take up his time for a bit. That's what I came to tell you.'

I relaxed slightly and so did Sheila.

'And how did you know we were here?' I asked.

'You forgotten that you sent Georgy Small to Mrs Breadwell when the filth was giving him trouble? I been cruising North Brom all evening looking out for you two.'

'We're very grateful to you, Warren,' I said. 'How long do you think you can stall your funny man?'

'About as long as it takes him or his mob to snuffle round London and find out the lady ain't there. But that won't be my fault, will it? After all, you managed to convince the Victoria that she's gone to London.'

He stood up. 'I shouldn't be hanging about here,' he said. 'Neither should you two. I'd get further away if I was you, Mr Tyroll.'

I nodded. 'Thanks again, Warren,' I said.

'Think nothing of it, Mr Tyroll. Like I said, you got to have loyalties, you got to stick to them as sticks to you. Tarra,' and he slipped out.

'Well!' exclaimed Sheila, as the door closed behind him. 'Is he for real?'

'He's very real,' I assured her. 'For all his bizarre and

unattractive politics, you have just met an old-fashioned member of the English working class, who's got a set of values that don't work any more – be grateful that he believes in the virtue of loyalty. At least we know we were right and we now know we've misled the opposition.'

'So what now?' she asked.

'Now we have a Gaelic coffee, you go back to Mrs Breadwell's and tomorrow we go and pay a visit to another potential witness. I'll pick you up around ten. Bring your Aussie Lady Bugger's Kit and your baggage.'

'Where are we off to?'

'When we've seen our witness, we're going to flee the country.'

I hate driving. It's such an appalling waste of time. You can't do anything else while you're driving, not even think about something else, or you end up dead. I learnt to drive in my youth and I've always tried to protect the public by not doing it, but I keep my licence for emergencies. This looked more and more like an emergency and I didn't want taxi-drivers and railway stations giving our movements away, so I borrowed a car from Claude the Phantom. Claude's real name is Gordon and he's a rarity among private enquiry agents because he's honest and bright. He got called 'Claude the Phantom' years ago, when he did a lot of divorce work and was always going about disguised as a gas inspector to gain access to adulterers' premises and see if there were men's socks in the lady's bedroom. Somehow we got to calling him 'Claude the Phantom' after Claude Rains as the *Phantom of the Opera*. When he's not enquiring he does socially useful tasks like repossessing unpaid-for cars, which means he's got contacts who've always got repo'd cars on hand, which means I can always borrow a car that's registered to someone else. Handy.

We had no trouble finding Sergeant Reynolds' place next morning, and his daughter-in-law took us into the garden to see him. It was warm and sunny and he was sitting reading under a mature apple tree. He stood up, with astonishing ease for a man of his age, as we walked down the lawn towards him. He was over six feet and showed no sign of an elderly stoop. As we got nearer I could see that his eyes were rheumy but he held his head erect. He motioned us to a cast-iron bench opposite his camp chair after I'd introduced us.

He sat back, eyeing Sheila thoughtfully. 'Walter Brown's granddaughter,' he repeated after a pause. 'That was a terrible thing that happened to him, terrible. And they haven't arrested anyone yet. In my day we used to say you have to catch a killer in forty-eight hours at most, and so we did. All the time I was in the old town force we never had a murder we didn't clear up. And it wasn't beaten out of them or done with faked papers. You know I knew your grandfather?' he said to Sheila.

'That's really why we came to see you,' I said. 'Dr McKenna's only here from Australia for a short time, just to put Mr Brown's affairs in order, and she's been trying to talk to anyone who knew him.'

'Oh yes, I knew him,' he said. 'I can't say we were great friends, because he was always a Labour Party man and a policeman has no politics, but we had quite a lot to do with each other, one way and another, him being at the Town Hall and me being the town centre sergeant for years. He used to get on to me about damage to corporation property, hooliganism and that. He was wicked with me about the school, when it was robbed. "Go and find 'em!" he said. "That's what Belston people pay their rates for!" Well, we solved all our murders, but some things got away from us, and that was one. It was bombed, you know, the Fountain Street School, and the Town Hall used the ruins for a store afterwards. Damned silly idea, if you ask me. I said to your grandfather, I said, "If you hadn't been keeping books in a damaged building they wouldn't have been stolen. 'Tis the Council's fault!" but he wouldn't let up on it. What he didn't know was that we had other orders, 'cos of the war. "Get on with what matters," we was told, "Leave it alone." So we did, didn't we?'

'Were you already a sergeant by the war?' asked Sheila.

'Oh yes, my dear. I joined the old Belston Town force just after the other war. You had to pass examinations then, and be six feet tall and have the eyesight. I never wanted to be a copper, though. If I'd had the chance I'd have been a footballer, but you had to get a steady job if you could and there wasn't the money in football them days. Do you know, when I heard I was accepted for the police, do you know what I did to celebrate?'

We shook our heads.

'I went to London for the Cup Final. Wolves was playing the Spurs. Beaten one-nil was the Wanderers. That was the year of the coal strike.'

'The General Strike?' asked Sheila.

'No, no. The miners were out on their own in '21. We had some rough old doings, I can tell you. Then we had it again in '26 with the General Strike. Course we had lots of pits about here then, lot of colliers, so we saw some action. I was going again, you know. I'd made up me mind to see the Cup Final again in '26. It was at Wembley by then. Bolton Wanderers was playing Manchester City. But I didn't get to go. It was only days before the strike and I never got away. We was all on stand-by.'

He looked into the past for a few moments, then turned to Sheila.

'I used to see your grandfather then, in the pub sometimes. He'd say, "Been out attacking strikers again, have you?" and I'd tell him, "No, but I've been out maintaining law and order and preserving the King's Peace." And we were.'

He smiled at the recollection. 'There was Bert Fray. He was a communist, always all over the place before the strike, winding up working people. We had orders to look at him a bit careful. Our bosses reckoned that when the strike started he'd be setting bombs, but that wasn't it at all. Just as the strike started he went and joined the Territorials. Well, his comrades was horrified, thought he'd betrayed them, joined the enemy.'

He chuckled. 'We had a big camp out on Cannock Chase, Territorial soldiers from all round the Black Country and police from all the towns. We was the reserve, ready to be rushed to wherever there was trouble. And there was trouble, here and there, but not so much as to need all the soldiers and police they'd got up at the camp. Most of the time we was putting out fires on the Chase. It was warm weather and every day the heath'd catch up there and we'd all be running about with brooms to put it out.'

His daughter-in-law materialised from the house with tea and biscuits. When it was distributed he carried on as though there had been no interruption.

'Well, one fine morning I was up early at our camp, taking a bit of a stroll before breakfast. I saw a soldier slipping out of his bell-tent and sliding into the trees. Now a good copper has an instinct, he knows when someone's up to something, and I was a good copper, though I says it meself. So I went after him, quiet like, and what do you think I found?'

We both shook our heads and he laughed.

'Comrade bloody Fray,' he said, 'off in the bushes with a box of Vestas, setting the heather on fire. That's what he'd been doing, every morning. Setting the Chase on fire so we'd be tied up putting it out and not go about bothering his comrades. Well, I had him and the magistrates gave him three months, the crafty little devil.'

He sipped his tea. 'But it wasn't all a chuckle,' he said. 'It went on, you know, after the General Strike, the miners stayed out when all the others had given up. There were some terrible things that summer.'

He fell silent, casting his mind back across the decades. 'You know the Belsich Road?' he asked me suddenly.

'Yes,' I said.

'There was a lot of pits up that way. After the General Strike was over there was hundreds of colliers and their families up around there – starving they were, that summer. They used to wait by the roadside, pitmen with pick-handles, and when a lorry came by they'd jump on it when it slowed for a corner or the canal bridge. They'd steal anything, but it was mostly food lorries, vegetables and that. The companies used to put chicken-wire on the windscreens to keep the stones off.'

He shook his head. 'We had to go out there and arrest 'em if we could. We had some bad fights up there, but we got numbers of them. I can't say I ever cared for locking up fellows who was only trying to feed their kids, but it had to be done. And there was a bright side. The pitmen couldn't get Relief while they was striking, but once we put 'em inside their families could go on the Relief. But they was bad times, bad all round,' and he shook his head again.

This was all fascinating stuff and another time I could have listened to him for days, but time wasn't on our side. I tried to steer the conversation, but he wasn't having it. Like Sergeant Crow had said, the memories were all there, but the old man's mind jumped about like a CD player. Piece by disordered piece he led us through the twenties and thirties. After another round of tea he was zigzagging into the forties.

I decided to focus things if I could. I put the Victory picture on the table. 'Do you remember the people in this picture?' I asked.

He reached out for it with one hand while the other fumbled in his shirt pocket for his spectacles. When they were in place he scanned the photo silently for some time.

'Well, well, my word. That's the back bar at the Eagle and Pump,' he said, after a while. 'Jim, the gaffer there, had a good football team going, you know, a team from the pub. We had a regular competition between the pubs. Lady Belston gave us a cup we used to play for. I was a bit past playing by then, but I used to coach the lads from the Bull. We had the cup the first three years it was played for.'

I tried to cut short the sporting reminiscences. 'So you know the people in the picture?' I asked.

'Oh, yes,' he said. 'Know them? I've nicked most of them, one time or another. That's the Cassidy brothers and their pals. When's this? It must be the end of the war. Good reason they had to be celebrating, they must have made ten fortunes over on the black market. There's Watson, and his oppo, Fred Thompson. They used to flog the stuff. Had a stall on the market for a while, taking bets and flogging black market gear. And there's Norman Berry, sharp dresser he was, always thought himself smarter than the average, and there's young Thorpe. Came to a sticky end, he did. I don't see the gaffer there, Jim's not in the picture.'

'We think the picture was taken from behind the bar,' I said.

'Ah,' he nodded. 'That'd be Jim, then, he was always one for

85

taking pictures. I've got loads of team photos as he took. The Eagle and Pump, the Engineers, the Station Hotel, the George, the Lamp Tavern, all of them. And the Bull of course, with the cup.'

He fell silent again for a while.

'But it stopped when the Bull was hit. That was when the second lot of flying bombs came in, the V2s. You could hear the old V1s, you had a bit of a chance. But them V2s, they just dropped straight down without a sound, then they went off.'

His eyes misted. 'That's what happened at the Bull. Broad daylight, lunchtime. Some said it was a stray bomber, but if it was God knows what he thought he was doing. Whatever it was it hit the Bull and that was it. Half the team gone in a flash. It knocked the heart out of us. We never had another game after that.'

He shook his head sadly. I feared he was about to drift into a reverie. 'What about Francy Cassidy?' I asked, which turned out to be a mistake.

'Francy Cassidy? He'd a been the smart one if he'd kept away from the women and the drink. He had the brains. But they most of 'em came to bad ends except him and Berry. He's still about, you know, Cassidy. He's in an old folks' home.'

'Not any more,' I said. 'He died just the other day.' I didn't give him the details. His pals on the force could do that in due course.

'Dead!' the old man exclaimed, and he gave a short barking laugh. 'Well, I never! So he's gone and I'm still here. But he was a crafty one, you know,' and he launched into his version of the copper theft.

'So we was never able to nick him for it,' he grumbled at the end. I was about to try and turn him back to the photograph, but a voice called down the lawn.

'Father, your lunch is ready.'

There was nothing to do but thank him and leave. As we walked down the side of the house I asked Sheila, 'Have you actually got all that on tape?'

'You betcha,' she said. 'Is any of it any use?'

'I don't know,' I said. 'Somewhere in it all there may be something. Look on the bright side. If it doesn't solve the case it'll get you a professorship in Black Country crime from 1920 to 1945.'

'It's going to be a hell of a job going through these tapes,' she said.

'That's one of the reasons we're going somewhere quiet,' I said. 'If we don't have to worry about the man in the sports jacket perhaps we can work out what the blazes is going on.'

'Where are we going?' she asked.

'Get in the car and I'll show you.'

14

'I've told you – I can't drive unless I'm thinking about driving and I can't think about other things if I'm driving.' I pointed the car west out of the conurbation and it was all right at first. Driving in traffic makes me concentrate, but once we got out of town my mind began to run on Sergeant Reynolds' ramblings. Was there something in it all that would help?

We had squeezed past a long line of lorries, each hauling a traveller's trailer, when Sheila suddenly put her hand on my knee, which didn't help my driving either.

'Chris,' she said, 'the object of this trip is to protect me, I gather?'

'Yes,' I replied. 'Somebody has killed two people over something and you look like a good bet for third place.'

'Right,' she said, slowly. 'Well, if you really want me to feel safe, can I ask you a favour?'

'Sure.'

'Will you pull up at the next lay-by and let me drive?'

I risked a glance at her. She looked quite serious. 'You can't,' I said.

'Do you know, you never struck me as a male chauvinist ocker,' she remarked, sharply.

'I'm not,' I said, 'whatever an ocker is. It's because you haven't got a UK driving licence and you don't know the way.'

'Do you know the way?' she demanded.

'Of course I do.'

'Right,' she commanded. 'Pull up and change places. You can see we get to the right place and I'll see we get there alive.'

So we did it her way. I slumped in the passenger seat and let my mind play detectives and Sheila drove us fast and skilfully. From time to time she asked for directions but otherwise we said very little.

We stopped for a late lunch in Shrewsbury and loaded up with groceries, before heading into Wales. By late afternoon we were deep in a remote part of the principality, winding along single-track roads flanked by hillsides thick with gnarled bushes.

'When we're over the hilltop,' I told her, 'you'll see a lake. Follow the road round the lake to the dam and turn left across the dam.'

The crest of the hill showed us the lake, gleaming in the late afternoon sun. Soon we were across the dam and turning right along another narrow track which wound up the face of a hill. Half a mile up I told her to pull off in front of a bungalow standing by itself.

Sheila climbed out and stretched and I followed her. 'Whose is this?' she asked. 'Yours?'

'No such luck,' I said. 'This belongs to the lovely Jayne. It was built for the manager when the dam went up, back in the fifties. Jayne's auntie bought it and thoughtfully died and left it to her.'

'And it has a road all of its own?' she asked.

I shook my head. 'There's a farm further up, around the shoulder of the hill.'

We humped our bags and the groceries indoors and I showed her the layout. Across the front of the two-bedroom bungalow Jayne's aunt had added a verandah that embraced the front bedroom and the sitting-room and gave a marvellous panorama of the lake. When I'd phoned Jayne and confirmed our safe arrival we made a meal and sat long on the verandah with a bottle of wine. Sheila took her grandfather's tin out and once again we spread out its contents and puzzled over them, but we got no further than the first time. Sergeant Reynolds' tapes we agreed to leave for the next day.

With a second bottle we simply sat, silent, watching the sun go down behind the hills beyond the lake. It became more and more difficult to believe the events of the last few days, and I kept looking at Sheila to convince myself she was real. We were only half-way through the bottle of wine when I began to believe that if she was, none of the rest mattered very much.

The mountains bring the dark early and soon it was growing chilly. Sheila shivered.

'It's too cold for a colonial from a hot country,' she said. 'What do people do in rural Wales after dark?'

'Well,' I said, 'there's not much on telly on a Saturday night and anyway the reception's rotten because of the mountains, so they either listen to the radio or go to bed.'

'Got a radio?' she asked.

'Only in the car,' I said.

'Not much of a place to take a nice, well-educated Aussie girl,' she said. 'We'll have to go to bed,' and she took my hand and we did.

Afterwards we lay in the lamplight and I admired her long, shapely back. 'You've got freckles all down your back,' I said, just for the sake of hearing her reply.

'That's the distinguishing mark of SA girls,' she said. 'New South Walers have bristles and West Australia girls have scales. Tell me, Mr Tyroll, before you get started again, isn't there a law against this?'

'We've got a lot of damn silly laws,' I said, 'but we haven't got one that stupid.'

'I thought you weren't supposed to do it with clients?' she said.

'You're not a client,' I said. 'Have I asked you for money?'

'Well, if I'm just a friend, you can do me a favour and fetch the ciggies from the verandah.'

I slipped out of bed and stepped out on to the verandah. The moon had risen and the lake was a sheet of silver under the black silhouette of the mountain opposite. I was turning back from the table with the cigarettes in my hand when something caught the edge of my vision.

Away across the moonlit lake the lights of vehicles were following the road by which we came. I turned back and watched them, puzzled and growing worried.

The flashing of the headlights through the lakeside bushes confused me, but once they turned on to the dam I could see there were two cars, still travelling in convoy.

'Chris,' Sheila called.

'Get dressed, quickly!' I said. 'I think we've got trouble.'

I dived back into the bedroom and dragged on a sweater and jeans while Sheila did the same.

'What's the panic?' she said.

'Stuff the holdalls!' I said. 'I think we've got visitors.'

I doused the lamp and slid back on to the verandah. I was right – the cars were turning off the dam in our direction and they weren't calling on a farmer at this time of night.

Back in the bedroom I grabbed Sheila by the arm. 'Out the back!' I said. 'I'll be right with you.'

We grabbed our overnight bags and Sheila dived out of the back door while I locked the front door and followed her, locking the rear door as I left.

Behind the bungalow was a small garden, fenced off from a wood that climbed across the upper slopes of the hill. By the time the two vehicles drew up in the lane we were into the fringe of the wood, sprawling in the bracken.

They parked just downhill of the bungalow and four men got out. Two of them were wearing some kind of dark uniform, but even at a distance and in the moonlight I didn't think they were police. The front car was a dark saloon and its occupants were both civilians. One was tall and wore a sports jacket and the other was slight with a black leather jacket.

They held some kind of conference in front of the second car, turning frequently to gesture at the bungalow. They must have been muttering for, despite the still night, not a sound of speech reached us. Then the four of them strolled slowly towards the house.

They stopped again, right in front of the house, and I waited for them to walk up and knock on the door with that middle-of-the-night knock that these people specialise in. I was disappointed.

Instead of knocking, the tall civilian pointed to each of the front windows and stepped back. His uniformed companions each swung their right arm and there was a loud sound of glass shattering in both windows. Seconds later Jayne's bungalow disappeared in a huge ball of orange flame that scorched our faces where we lay.

15

They knew! The bastards knew, or they thought they knew, that we were asleep in that bungalow, and they torched it as easy as swatting a fly. Sheila huddled in my arms and shook with shock and I held her closely, not just to comfort her but because I was shaking just as badly. It was like watching yourself being murdered.

Whatever the bombers had used was very efficient. After that first huge double explosion of flame the bungalow had caved in on itself and burned fiercely. Already the fire was dying down and it was possible to see that there was precious little left of Jayne's inheritance.

I peered past the flames, looking for the vehicles, but they had already disappeared and I spotted their lights flickering on the far side of the lake.

'They've gone,' I said.

'What are they going to do?' Sheila whispered.

'Go home and celebrate, I imagine,' I said. 'They think they've just cremated us both.'

'What are we going to do?'

'Camp out till daylight, then take the car.'

'Can't we go now?'

'I don't fancy going the way they've gone and I don't think

we can find our way through these lanes in the dark. We'd better leave it till the morning.'

'Then where'll we go?'

'Good question,' I said, and I hadn't the least idea of an answer.

Time was when the idea of a summer night in a ferny wood with a beautiful woman would have sent my pulse racing. Not any more. It was chilly and we were already cold with shock. God invented bracken for badgers to sleep on, not people. We just lay, cold, frightened and uncomfortable and mostly unsleeping until the sky beyond the trees turned grey. Much of the time I was thinking about Sheila's last question.

As twilight comes early between the hills, so dawn comes late. Chilled and damp by the time the birds began to sing, we still had to wait for the sun to rise over the mountains.

'Morning,' I said, when I was sure that Sheila was awake. 'You haven't, by any chance, got any food in your wonder bag? The odd freeze-dried wombat or a fistful of witchetty grubs would go down very nicely just now.'

She stretched herself and winced. 'There's some choc bars in my holdall,' she said, and began looking for them. 'I could do with a brew-up though.'

'No such luck,' I said, 'but there's a flask of whisky in the front pocket of my bag.'

We breakfasted, Sheila gagging after a swallow from the flask.

'You really know how to give a girl a good time, Chris. A romantic night under the stars and a first-class malt for breakfast. What's next?'

'Trying to find somewhere to hole up without getting killed, I suppose.'

I slipped the flask into my pocket and we picked up the bags and began to make our way down to the lane. The sun was up and the air was warming. Mist was rising off the lake.

I hobbled across Jayne's garden. The uncomfortable night had not done my grazed leg any good. We came along the side of the wreckage, now smoking silently, and stepped on to the road. I could see our car, still where we had left it, seemingly unharmed. Its bright colour and mechanical ordinariness were welcome signs of sanity in a world that had gone crazy.

Then two bullets hummed past us and a silenced pistol plopped twice. I dropped my bag, spun round and cannoned into Sheila. As we stumbled together another bullet sang past.

'Get back!' I snapped. 'There's one of them in our car!'

Sheila sprinted and I hobbled as fast as I could back across the garden and into the trees. Breathlessly we fell back into our old lair.

We could see both sides of the bungalow and no one seemed to be following us, but, as we recovered our breath, we heard the crackle of a shortwave radio.

'We can't stay here,' I told Sheila. 'He's calling reinforcements.'

'Where to?' she asked.

I tried to recall the map and journeys made on previous visits to Jayne's bungalow.

'If we go on up the slope,' I said, 'we can drop down the other side of the hill. There's a road there.'

'Can't we head along to this farm you talked about?'

I shook my head. 'They'll come after us anywhere and I don't want to lead them to anyone else. God knows what they'd do to the farm after what they did last night.'

We stuffed our pockets with what we could from the holdalls and set out up through the wood. It was hard going. Once past the edge of the trees the undergrowth was thick and some of it was thorny. When, eventually, we reached the far edge, we paused to gasp, sweat and listen for any sound of pursuit. We couldn't hear anything.

'He's not following,' said Sheila, hopefully.

'He doesn't have to. He can sit and wait for his back-up. But he knows we haven't gone down on to the dam road so we're either in the woods or making for the next valley. They'll try and cut us off.'

After another quick slug from the flask we began the next stage, a scramble across steep grassy slopes, patched with tumbles of boulders. I had stopped noticing whether my left leg still hurt. All the rest of me did now.

The sun was now well up and we were drenched in sweat by the time we reached the summit. Making our way to the far side we collapsed against a large boulder and scanned the landscape below. There was no tree cover on this side of the hill and we could see all the way down to a narrow road running along the valley bottom.

The sun flashed on something beside the road and my eyes picked out two vehicles parked beside the stream. We were too late. One of the vehicles was a dark green transit van and even as we watched it began to disgorge a group of men in dark uniforms.

There was nothing to say. We dropped out of sight behind the rocks and lay, each of us silently cursing. At last Sheila lit a cigarette and passed me one.

She rolled over and peered down between the boulders.

'They've spread out,' she reported. 'They're moving up in a line across.'

'Then we're sunk,' I said. 'We're surrounded.'

'There's only one bloke behind us,' she said.

'How do we know? There was only one this morning, but he's the bloke who called up the big battalions. What's the betting he's got reinforcements by now?'

We smoked in silence. At last she threw away her cigarette end and said, 'Well, we can't go down that way. It's all open and they'd see us a mile off. We'll just have to go back.'

'Where we know there's at least one bloke with a gun and maybe half a dozen more? What's the point?'

'The point', she said, 'is that there are trees behind us. If we stay here they just herd us in like sheep. If we go back we've got a bit of cover, right down to the road by the dam. If we can give them the slip in the woods they'll all be up here when we hit the road,' and she looked at me expectantly.

I was tired and sore and depressed. It was only because I was also frightened of being killed that I didn't just lie there till they came for us.

'OK,' I said, reluctantly. 'Let's give it a try.'

So we scrambled back down towards the tree-line, every moment expecting the uniforms to emerge from the woods and trap us in the open, but we made the trees unmolested. There we halted to listen.

They cheat in the movies. When people slink about in jungles and forests there's no sound-track so it's all creepy and silent. In real life it's extremely difficult to move silently in thick woodland. The noise of movement was going to be our worst enemy, but there was an up side. If they could hear our movements, we could hear theirs. We listened hard and heard nothing, so we began a stealthy attempt to slip through those wretched tangled thickets in silence.

We had made about a hundred yards when I pulled Sheila down and dropped beside her.

'Listen!' I hissed. 'There's a swishing noise.'

We strained our ears again. I was right. From at least two places, right and left ahead of us, came a rhythmic swishing noise.

'Nice of them,' whispered Sheila. 'They're beating the bush for us. Blowing a bugle would have been better, but at least we know where they are.'

'Great,' I said. 'They're too bloody close together. We'll never get between them without them hearing.' An idea occurred to me. 'Look,' I said, 'if we stay here until they're closer, then I'll run at the left-hand one, very noisily. The right-hand one will join in if I make enough fuss.'

'And what do I do?' she hissed.

'As soon as I've drawn them off, you slip away through the gap to the right and keep going to the road.'

'No way,' she said. 'You'll get shot the minute they hear you and I'll end up raped and shot in a Welsh jungle. No thank you, counsellor.'

'Got any better ideas?'

'Didn't we jump a stream on the way up?'

'Yes, it's a bit ahead of us. They must still be the other side. What are you thinking?'

'I don't know,' she said. 'It's a barrier and it'll make the going easier.'

She got up cautiously and I followed her as she began moving forward again. In another twenty yards we came to the stream, a narrow trickle between shallow banks. Sheila was right, by walking in the water we could make better speed with no more noise, but as we moved away to the right I wondered how many men were between us and the road.

Following the stream downhill we paused every few minutes to listen. The swishing was growing nearer and there were more than two beaters, but the banks of the stream were growing higher and might provide more cover.

The fifth or sixth time we stopped to listen the sound of beating was very close and we could hear the occasional snap of a twig under the beater's foot.

'It's no good,' I said. 'They're almost on top of us and there's still nowhere to hide. We'd better climb up on the bank and try my idea.'

'No way,' she said again and, as she did so, a hand fell on my shoulder.

16

I didn't cry out, but only because my heart was blocking my throat as I spun round.

Ankle-deep in the stream stood a boy of about fourteen, with grubby suntanned features under ill-kempt brown hair. He was dressed in well-worn brown denims and gumboots. At first I didn't recognise him.

'Mr Tyroll,' he said, speaking fast and low. 'They're almost here. Come with me now,' and he started away down the stream as soon as he had finished speaking, pulling me after him by the arm.

He led us confidently and silently, always stepping where there was sand rather than gravel under water and never making a splash as he walked. He led us round a sharp bend in the stream and as we turned the corner we heard the noise of rushing water.

The boy turned back to us. 'There's a waterfall,' he said,

pointing ahead. 'There's a pool underneath it. Drop into the pool and there's a big slab where the water splashes. If you climb out on that you'll see a hole at the back of the waterfall. They'll never see you if you're in there.'

'What'll you do?' I said. 'They're killers.'

'I'll be OK,' he said, nonchalantly. 'Nobody'll see me in the woods. Stay in the hole and I'll come for you when they've gone,' and he sprang up the bank and vanished into the undergrowth.

There was no time to lose. At the brink of the fall we could see that it dropped about fifteen feet. Clasping hands we dropped into the pool.

The water was chest-deep, enough to cushion our fall, but I slid on the sloping bottom of the pool and went right under. When I surfaced I found Sheila standing beside me, dragging me to my feet with one hand while the other held her indispensable shoulder-bag clear of the water.

'If you've had your swim,' she said, 'there's the hidey-hole,' and she pointed to a large, flat slab that formed a splashboard at the base of the waterfall.

Quickly we scrambled on to it. Close to the fall we could see a shadow behind it and, when we plunged through the watery screen, we found a deep vertical slit in the rock. Slipping inside we found that it was just big enough for two people to perch on outcrops in its sides.

'Could have been made for two,' observed Sheila.

'Maybe it was,' I said, pointing to old cigarette butts on the moist floor.

'Good-oh,' she said. 'I'm glad smoking's permitted. I could just do with a smoke.'

She delved into her repository and produced cigarettes and a lighter, which reminded me of the flask in my pocket. Nicotine and alcohol brought our pulses back to normal and restored our flagging energy. I looked at my companion. She had been firebombed, shot at, chased up and down a mountain and had jumped down a waterfall and there she sat, dripping water, flushed and tousled, but every inch as desirable as when she first walked into my office.

97

She intercepted my gaze. 'No time for that,' she said.

'We've nothing else to do.' I grinned. 'Not till Martin gets back, anyway.'

She pulled me across to her and kissed me, long and hard. 'That'll have to do for now,' she said as we disengaged. 'Now come clean. Who's the kid and how does he know you?'

'He's the son of an old client of mine, but I'd no idea he was hereabouts.'

'Thank your stars he was,' she said. 'We weren't going to get out of that mess in a hurry.'

Above the rush of falling water I heard a voice calling, 'Mr Tyroll, Mr Tyroll.' Sheila grabbed her bag and we plunged back through the fall.

Our guide was outside, squatting at the side of the slab, his impish brown features lit with a wide grin.

'They've gone,' he reported. 'They're way up the slope now. How d'you like the little hidey-hole?'

'Fine,' I said, 'but where have you been?'

'I just went up a tree, sir. They was looking in the bushes and all about them all the time. They never thought to look up.'

He looked around him. 'We'd better be going, sir. They'll soon find out they've missed you.'

'Lead on,' I said, 'but where are we going?'

'Me daddy said to bring you to him,' he said and jumped down to the side of the stream.

He set off downwater and we followed. From the pool below the little fall the stream ran on between high banks. Soon we were in a deep, narrow cleft, completely overhung by trees. When our path swung left I began to realise where we were. I recalled the little bridge on the mountain road and a stream that flowed into the reservoir above the dam.

Sure enough, in a moment Martin left the stream's course and clambered agilely up the side of the cleft to our right, waiting at the top for us to follow.

He struck off through the trees and soon we were at the fence dividing the wood from open meadows. We trotted after him down the narrow margin between the trees and the fence. At the bottom of the field the fence met a dry-stone wall that flanked the road. Here there was a gate in the wall and leaning on the gate was a figure in amorphous tweeds with a shapeless tweed hat. As we clambered through the fence and emerged into the field the figure raised its hat and called out.

'Good-day to you, Mr Tyroll! And to you, miss.'

I turned to Sheila. 'Dr McKenna,' I said, 'permit me to introduce Mr Patrick Murphy, traveller, tarmac-layer, scrap-dealer and singer. Good-day to you, Paddy.'

He nodded to Sheila and looked us over, narrowly.

'You'll be wanting to get dry,' he said, 'and to be out of sight before them fellas find out you're not up there.'

He turned away through the gate and we followed him as he ambled along the road. A hundred yards or so ahead there was a stretch of ground between the road and the lake, and there we could see a clutch of trailers and lorries parked. The little black chimneys of the caravans revealed that they belonged to travellers, not holiday-makers.

In the middle of the camp a fire burned and a handful of Paddy's companions, male and female, were sitting about it on upturned boxes, picnic chairs and, in one case, an old-fashioned wooden rocking-chair. Children of all ages from toddlers to early teens played around the group and between the trailers. Many of the adult faces I recognised and several of them smiled at my appearance.

'Hello there, Mr Tyroll,' one young man called. 'Are you having a spot of bother with the police, then?'

I grinned back at him and Paddy responded. 'They're not the police,' he said. 'They're private guards. Now then, Mr Tyroll and the young lady need some dry clothes, can you find some out for them?'

He turned away to a trailer and we followed him into it. Sheila gaped at the interior. Travellers' trailers are made by the firms that build holiday caravans, but the travelling people have them made to order, paying for a number of extras that they consider essential.

To our right as we stepped on board was an elaborately fitted kitchen, filling the wide, bowed end of the vehicle. Upholstered seats ran along from the kitchen, interrupted on one side by a squat coke stove. Beyond the stove were more seats, opening out into the far end, where a richly decorated seat, heaped with embroidered cushions, ran round under the windows. Every horizontal surface was covered in Formica and most of the vertical surfaces were concealed behind tinted mirrors with cut-glass decoration at their edges. Bobbled curtains dressed the windows and a narrow shelf ran round the whole interior, filled with Royal Doulton china and items in red and blue cut glass.

Our host showed us into the far bay, pulled an old mackintosh from a cupboard and flung it over the seats.

'There you are,' he said. 'Sit yourselves on that while we get you something to wear. You must be dropping,' and he went out again, beckoning his son after him.

I spread the old mac wide and both of us dropped our wet, exhausted persons gratefully on to the couch. I wrapped an arm around Sheila and pulled her to me. She chuckled, quietly.

'I just don't believe any of this,' she said. 'Who are Paddy and the boy and those people? They live like gypsies, but they don't look like them.'

'They're Irish travellers,' I explained. 'All over Britain you'll find travellers. The gypsies are latecomers, they got here from India about five hundred years ago, but Paddy's people were already here.'

She shook her head, wonderingly. 'What do we do now?' she said.

'It's Paddy's show,' I said. 'He seems to have something in mind. We can't run and we daren't fight, so I guess he's thinking of a way to hide us again.'

Paddy returned with an armful of clothing and towels. 'Here,' he said. 'You can put them on. Do you need a separate place, miss, to dress?'

'What? Oh, no,' said Sheila. 'He's already seen anything I've got to show.'

'I thought that might be it,' said Paddy, and winked at me. He pulled a folding partition across the trailer which cut off the end we were sitting in, and left us to it.

100

When he tapped the partition a few minutes later we had rubbed ourselves dry and changed clothes. He looked us over critically. Both of us were in jeans that fitted well enough. I had a check shirt and Sheila wore a tight purple sweater that did wonders for her figure. Both of us were barefoot and our own footgear was sopping wet.

Paddy rummaged in a cupboard and passed me a pair of battered gumboots, then peered closely at Sheila's feet.

'Martin,' he called to his son, 'come here and give us your boots!'

The boy ducked past his father, dropped on the couch and kicked off his gumboots, exposing bare brown feet. Paddy picked up the boots and passed them to Sheila.

'Try them,' he commanded.

Without batting an eyelid, Sheila pulled them on, rolled the tops down and tucked her jeans into them. Paddy eyed us again, then dipped his hand into a drawer and pulled out a handful of bangles and necklaces.

'There's some of the missus' stuff,' he said to Sheila. 'You need a lot to look like a traveller woman.'

When she had hung herself about with the decorations he gave us his final inspection.

'You're fair enough to pass for a traveller,' he said to Sheila. 'You,' he said to me, 'are too dark for a traveller. You're black enough to be a Romany, but they wouldn't know the difference.' He thought for a moment. 'You need a hat,' he said, and another plunge into a cupboard produced a snap-brim brown felt which was only slightly too big.

'That's it,' he said, at last.

'What next?' I asked.

'Well now, I don't know who them fellas as was chasing you are, but they seemed like hard men. When they find you're not up on that hill they'll come looking for you and the first place they'll come is here. Now they won't be looking for you, 'cos they wouldn't think we'd take you in, but they'll ask if we've seen you.'

'Are all your people OK, Paddy?' asked Sheila.

'My people know Mr Tyroll well,' he said, 'and he's always been for us when others was against us. They know what to say.'

'What do you want us to do?' I asked. 'Stay in here?'

'No, no,' he said. 'They might start poking about and it'd look bad. Come outside and join in with the people. Just remember – if they come here, don't lift your eyes to them. Travellers don't look police and their like in the eyes.'

He led us out of the trailer, to a chorus of friendly chaff from the people standing about and wide-eyed stares from the children.

A young man I recognised grinned at me and clapped me on the shoulder. 'I knew it,' he said. 'I always thought you was one of us at heart, Mr Tyroll!'

Paddy was still directing the performance. He borrowed a baby for Sheila to hold and sat her down among the women and girls by the fire, then took me to a battered van that had its bonnet up, calling its owner over.

'You two just look as if you're fixing it!' he commanded and left us.

He had set the scene just in time. A column of vehicles, the familiar blue car at the front, came down the hill and drew up on the road above us. Twenty or so of the uniformed men dropped out of two vans and our two civilian friends emerged from the car. They advanced purposefully towards the camp and Paddy, a small dog snuffling at his heels, strolled up towards them.

The tall fair man spoke to Paddy, though I couldn't hear what was said. While he did so the uniformed men spread past them and came among the travellers. The travellers were completely passive, simply stepping aside to let them pass and only turning to watch silently as the uniforms went from trailer to trailer, opening doors and peering inside. Paddy's people had a lifetime of experience in this kind of situation.

I kept my head well down over the van's exposed engine and prayed silently. Suddenly I felt that uneasy prickle that tells you you're the subject of someone's attention.

I risked a cautious glance upwards under the brim of my hat.

Two uniformed men stood at the centre of the camp, looking around, and one of them had fixed his gaze on me and my companion. They began to walk towards us.

'Look down!' my traveller friend hissed, and pointed into the engine.

It took all the nerve I had to drop my eyes to the engine again, but as I did so I heard a noise. It was the sound of a car, coming down the hill at high speed.

One of the uniforms shouted and now I did look up. Everyone, travellers and intruders, was looking towards the road and I followed their gaze.

The car which we had left parked by the burnt-out cottage was coming down the hill, barrelling down the narrow road. At the junction of the dam road it swung into a sliding, screeching turn and hurtled out along the dam, trailing blue smoke.

The spell broke. Orders were shouted and our visitors raced for their vehicles. In seconds all of their vehicles were tearing out on to the dam in hot pursuit, but their quarry was already almost out of their sight on the far side.

I wiped my sweating face with my forearm and felt the tension drain out of me. Paddy strolled across and, lifting his hat, scratched his balding head with the same hand.

'I think that's the last we'll be seeing of the queer fellas,' he remarked, conversationally.

'Who the blazes was in the car?' I asked.

'That was my eldest, Miley and his girl. He's always taking motors for the devilment, so I told him to make himself useful for a change.'

'They're dangerous men, Paddy,' I said. 'I hope he'll be all right.'

'Ah, he'll be just fine. He's run most of the police in England and Wales and the army in Belfast so I doubt these fellas will do any good with him. Now then, you'll be wanting something to eat.'

17

'Right then, Paddy. We've told you our end of the story – now how come you knew where we were and what was happening, and anyway, where's Cathleen?'

We had dined, crudely but extremely satisfyingly, on huge sandwiches of boiled bacon and mugs of bright orange tea liberally splashed with Jamesons. With food and security, however temporary, the fears from the firebombing and the hunt through the woods were receding and curiosity was taking their place.

Paddy smiled his slow, toothy grin at my question.

'Well now,' he said, 'Cathleen's Mammy is sick in Manchester and she's away down to see her and she's got the young ones with her, so there's just me and Miley and Martin and I thought I'd come into Wales and have a bit of hunting and fishing.'

'Poaching!' I accused.

'So you say,' he said. 'We was on the way up here yesterday and I saw you two in a car that passed us. Then, when we set our camp here I went for a bit of a stroll after dark, just taking the air like. I saw your car again, up by the little house, and I thought it was handy in case I was needing a lawyer. I was up in the woods there, just minding my business and enjoying the fresh air, when them queer fellas came along and did their dirty business.'

He paused and splashed more whiskey into his tea before taking a long draught.

'When I saw that fire, I thought you was gone, so I did, Mr Tyroll. I didn't stay there after that. There's nothing scares a traveller like fire, you know.'

'Travellers aren't the only ones,' Sheila remarked.

'Then,' said our host, 'I got to thinking this morning that I just ought to find out what had happened to you, so I sent young Martin up to look. He said you was both on the run up the hill and the queer fellas was behind you, so I sent him to go back and find you and show you that little hidey place under the water.'

'You've saved us twice today,' I said. 'I owe you, Paddy.'

'Not at all,' he said. 'You've always been a help to me and my people. You've stood up for us when no one else would do anything but spit on us. You owe me nothing.'

There was an embarrassed silence for moments and we all drank to cover it, then Paddy said, 'And you really don't know who them fellas are?'

We shook our heads.

'They're not wobs,' he said.

'Wobs?' repeated Sheila.

'Coppers,' I translated, 'scuffers, fuzz, filth, the Old Bill, whatever you call them. The travellers call them "wobs". It's back-slang for Bows – Bow Street Runners.'

She stared at me as if she couldn't believe she was drinking with a man who used Regency street-slang. 'Actually,' she said, 'we call them "blue-heelers" – for Peelers. But if they're not coppers, what are they?'

'Miley says they're private guards from some big company,' said Paddy.

'Private security!' I exclaimed, then a thought struck me. 'I suppose they might be from Kerrenwood's. Their plants have their own security men and they're all over the country. No wonder they could whistle up reinforcements in Wales.'

'Why Kerrenwood's?' demanded Sheila. 'When I suggested them before, you put it down.'

'I didn't know there was private security involved then,' I said. 'I thought it was only two men.'

'Do you have private security firms in Britain who kill people?' she asked. 'I've read about your nuclear police, but I thought Kerrenwood's security boys would just be guarding their factories and stopping thieving.'

'Mac mentioned an old lady in Shropshire who was murdered a few years ago. There's a strong suspicion that she was killed by a private firm under contract to some secret branch of the government. It can happen,' I said.

'But what's the connection between Kerrenwood's and the funnies?' she asked. 'Why're they doing the dirty work?'

'It looks like whatever your grandfather was looking into means a lot to Kerrenwood's. It can damage them badly in some way. Lord Kerrenwood's a pal of those in power – an old, valuable pal, with pots of money. If Walter Brown looked like making trouble for Kerrenwood's then there's been a trading of favours.'

'But what the blazes did Grandpa and Francy Cassidy know that's such a threat to Kerrenwood's?'

The spirit was rapidly eating into my tired brain. 'Just now I haven't the least idea,' I said. 'Ask me tomorrow.'

'You'll be wanting to turn in,' said Paddy. 'Use this place for your own.'

'We can't turn you out,' Sheila protested, but he grinned. 'I've three trailers,' he said. 'One for the young ones, one for cooking and that, and this one for best. I'll squeeze in with the boys. Goodnight to you,' and he was gone.

The couch in the bay converted into a magnificent double bed and in minutes we were under a pile of quilts. I had just closed my eyes when Sheila said, 'Chris?'

'Yes,' I murmured.

'I think I love you,' and she kissed me long and softly as I slid away into a dreamless sleep.

We woke as soon as the sun lit the windows just above our heads. Martin must have been on orders to watch for our rising because, minutes after we had dressed, he was at the door with large breakfasts and more mugs of strong tea. His father was not far behind and I was relieved to see that he was accompanied by a grinning Miley.

'They didn't catch you, then?' I said to the older lad.

'Me? Not a chance!' he said. 'We gave them a run about in the hills for a bit, then we went to a station and left the car there. We got a train for Shrewsbury, got off it there and hitched a ride back. They'll be thinking you've gone home.'

'That was clever,' I said. 'I was worried about you.'

'Not at all,' he scoffed. 'I've had it away from them fellas more than once.'

'Really?' I said. 'Who do you think they were?'

106

'I know who they are,' he said. 'I've run them a time or two. They was private guards – you know, security men.'

'So it is private security,' exclaimed Sheila.

'Warren said that the man who blackmailed him to find you was official,' I recollected. 'What's he doing using a private army? Why isn't he using Special Branch? They're supposed to back up the security service when there's mayhem afoot.'

'Perhaps the Special Branch have a rule about not murdering people in their beds,' she said, sarcastically.

'Maybe you're right,' I said, and maybe she was, but I wasn't best pleased to learn we were up against some kind of unofficial unholy alliance.

After breakfast we split up. I needed to contact the office but the mobile phone had been incinerated and, in any case, it had occurred to me that it was the way in which we had been traced. My call to Jayne had given the hunters our location. I got Paddy to drive me to a phone box, well away from the camp in case they'd taken the precaution of bugging the local ones. For the same reason I couldn't call the office direct, but I reckoned it was safe to speak to Claude the Phantom. He could carry my messages in and out of the office without attracting attention.

Sheila stayed behind and set to work listening to her tapes of Sergeant Reynolds' ramblings. When Paddy and I got back she had nearly completed the task and was taking a tea-break. She had set out on the table the contents of her grandfather's tin and was gazing at them reflectively. Martin sat on the floor by her, watching her with wide brown eyes.

I kissed the top of her head and murmured, 'The boy's in love with you and I don't blame him.'

'Nonsense,' she whispered. 'He's just making sure I don't make off with his gumboots!'

Paddy joined us and looked at the display on the table. He picked up one of the cards.

'I haven't seen one of them for a day or two,' he said and showed it to Martin. 'Look there,' he said, 'that's an identity card. When the war was on you all had to have one of them to prove you wasn't a German spy.'

'Were you around then?' I asked, because Paddy's age was a matter of conjecture and his stories went back to prehistory.

'Oh, yes,' he replied. 'I was here. Of course, I was only a bit of a tiddler then, but I remember those cards, and the ration books. I remember one time me daddy had a fella staying with us who hadn't a card or a ration book. Something to do with him not wanting to be a soldier or something like that. They was going along one day, me daddy driving and this fella alongside him, and they run into the soldiers with guns. They had the road blocked and was checking people's cards.'

'What did they do?' I asked.

'Well, a soldier comes to the window of the van and asked me daddy for his card and he gives it to him. "Who's that with you?" he says, meaning the queer fella. "That's me eldest son," says me daddy, and he takes the card back and puts it in the other fella's pocket. Well, the soldier steps round the van and asks the other fella for his card. "With pleasure," he says and takes me daddy's card out of his pocket. Well, of course, they weren't surprised that the names were the same, so they let them go.' He chuckled reflectively as we laughed. 'He was a quick-thinking fella was me daddy, God bless him.'

'Did you manage to make anything out of Sergeant Reynolds' memoirs?' I asked Sheila.

She shook her head. 'I've scribbled on every piece of paper in my bag and Martin got me some more, but none of it seems to tie up. The only really new thing we've got is the name of the guy who took the piccy – Jim the landlord. I don't really think that helps much.'

We went over her notes. We compared them with the notes from our talk with little Mrs Cassidy, but we had no blinding insights. In the end we gave it up and went for a dip in the lake.

The water, fed from mountain streams, was ice-cold even in midsummer but we found ways to warm ourselves when we came out. Afterwards we sat and watched a hot red sun slide down behind the hills. Soon it was dark and a little breeze began to flick the surface of the reservoir.

'Listen,' I said. 'You can hear the bells if you listen closely.'

'What bells?'

'There's two villages under the lake. They were flooded in the fifties when the dam was built. The Welsh say you can hear the church bells from one of them when the wind blows.'

'Really?' she said. 'That's sad, that poor little church, down in the depths, ringing for services and nobody comes.'

'If I didn't know better,' I said, 'I'd think you were a real softy.'

'Oh, I am,' she said. 'I am,' and pulled me into a clinch. 'Tell you what,' she whispered in my ear, 'if I ask you to marry me, can we do it down there? A scuba wedding like they have at Surfers Paradise?'

'Yes,' I said, instantly. 'If we can find a Welsh vicar with a wetsuit you're on, but one of us is going to do a lot of commuting.'

'No worries.' She smiled. 'We'll think of something, Chris.'

Some time later we strolled hand in hand back to the camp. A few people still sat by the fire in the darkness and Paddy was crooning one of his old songs to them, but I wanted to preserve the moments by the lake so we bade them goodnight and turned in.

It can't have been five minutes after I had turned out the gas mantle over our bunk when Sheila sat up and started to grab about in the dark on the floor.

'What are you doing?' I complained.

'Put the light on,' she commanded. 'I've got an idea.'

I groped for the matches on the window-sill and relit the gas. She had dragged her bag on to the bed and got Walter Brown's tin out.

'It was that tale of Paddy's,' she explained. 'About two blokes using one identity card. It's not that, but it's something like it.'

She had taken out the two ration books and was leafing through the one for James Brown.

'What do those mean?' she demanded, and showed me a page with rubber-stamped addresses on it.

'You had to register,' I said. 'For certain goods you had to be registered with a supplier, a grocer, a butcher and so on. Why?'

'Because this isn't Great Uncle Jim's ration book, that's why!' she announced triumphantly. 'He was in Nottingham all through the war. Look at those addresses – they're all Belston shops. He didn't travel sixty miles every time he wanted his two ounces of butter. This is some other James Brown's ration book.'

My mind was beginning to work again. 'You're right,' I said, 'but what does that mean?'

'Don't you see?' she said. 'Grandpa kept a picture of blokes with ration books that he thought was significant. He also kept a ration book that belonged to someone called James Brown. He knew it wasn't his brother's. He must have thought that was significant too. It's all about ration books!'

'The black market?' I queried. 'That can't be worth killing people about fifty years on, can it?'

'I don't know,' she said, 'but it's about ration books and I'll tell you something else – I bet Jim Brown was the bloke that took the picture. Where else did Grandpa get it?'

18

I woke in the grey pre-dawn light next morning and lay, smoking and trying to think it all through. I kept getting confused by the recollection that I had promised to marry the beautiful girl who slept quietly beside me. I had one short, brutal marriage behind me – to a fellow law student who believed that marrying a promising young solicitor was an easier route to a life of luxury than practising her profession. It worked just long enough for us to get out of law school and for me to go to work – for the wrong firm. Suddenly the scales fell from her eyes and she saw that I couldn't care less about property law or commercial law or tax avoidance or any of those things that pay for designer goodies for lawyers' wives, that I was actually interested in trying to achieve a little justice for people. When that happened she took off – with the car, the best of the furniture, the statuette from the hall that Daddy bought us and the junior partner in a commercial practice, with whom she has been expensively and maliciously unhappy ever since.

Now, here I was about to try again, and where was here? A travellers' camp in Wales, outside which were a brace of psychopaths and an unspecified number of hired thugs who had now proved several times that someone preferred Sheila and me dead. It looked like an even worse beginning than the first time round.

The first rays of light woke the birds, who woke the camp bantams, who woke the camp dogs, who woke the camp children, who woke their mothers and suddenly it sounded like the Battle of the Somme outside the trailer. Sheila woke and rolled over, smiling at me in a way that made the whole ridiculous mess seem much more probable.

'Good-day, counsellor,' she said. 'Penny for 'em?'

'I was just wondering', I said, 'if you really meant it, last night.'

'If you mean the marrying bit,' she said, pulling me into an embrace, 'the answer's yes. My head of department back home says that when a girl finds a good man she ought to shoot him and have him stuffed before he goes off. You look like you've got the makings to me, Chris Tyroll, so I guess you're stuck with it,' and she wrapped herself so entirely around me I couldn't have argued if I'd wanted to.

When I surfaced I said, 'There was the other bit as well – the brainwave.'

'The thingy books? The ration books?' she queried. 'That's just got to be part of the answer, Chris. There's no other reason why Grandpa had the picture and some other fellow's book. There's some kind of connection – there's got to be.'

I nodded. 'The only thing is', I said, 'that everyone was into the black market then. How could it matter so much now that they'll kill for it?'

111

'Perhaps they killed then,' she said. 'Remember – a couple of those blokes in the picture came to sticky ends. One went into a canal and another ended up knifed in an alley – unsolved. Two of them just melted away, didn't they? Maybe there's a very old murder or two in this.'

'Could be,' I agreed. 'We've never checked out Norman Berry.' I told her about my attempts to track him from the phone book. 'Look,' I said, coming to a sudden decision, 'we can't do anything about it while we're here. I'm going back to the Midlands.'

She pulled away from me. 'You're going back? What do I do? Stay here and get on with my embroidery like a good little girl?'

'Hold on a minute. Miley misled the baddies into thinking we'd gone back. By now they must have scoured Belston and district for us and they'll be pretty sure we're not there. So they're going to try and pick up the trail where they lost it – here. Paddy and his folk can't disappear completely and I'd hate to be responsible for those thugs cutting loose on this camp. If I appear back in Belston, they won't touch me because they want to find you. Meanwhile I'll have a better chance of finding out what the piccy means. Make sense?'

She grimaced. 'I suppose it does, but I don't like it, Chris. How can we keep in touch?'

'You can ring Claude the Phantom's answering machine every day. Give it a callbox number and I'll call you there at seven.'

Grudgingly she muttered her agreement, then dragged me back into an embrace. Later she whispered, 'Look after yourself, Chris Tyroll. You've got some very nice bits I'd like to keep.'

Over breakfast I outlined the plan to Paddy. He said little, but his slow nod showed his agreement. 'Never fear,' he said, 'we'll look after the lady. By the way,' he continued, 'Queenie says she'd like to see the pair of you.'

We followed him across the ring of the little camp to another large trailer on the other side. It was the same make as Paddy's, but brocaded velvet drapes darkened every window. Paddy knocked at its door and waited until a female voice called us in.

'If you think Paddy's trailer is something,' I whispered to Sheila, 'just wait till you get in here.'

There was no kitchen area in the big trailer. At the far end, the bedroom area was closed off with heavy drapes and the near-end bow had been turned into a permanent sitting-room. It was lavishly furnished with embroidered cushions and the floor underfoot was thick with decorative rugs. The only light came from small gas-burners in coloured glasses, whose light sparkled off shelves of gold-ornamented Royal Doulton china and deep ruby cut-glass ware.

On a rocking-chair in the midst of this splendour sat Queenie Connors, matriarch of Paddy's tribe, ninety years old if she was a day and maybe much more. Still tall, despite her years, she was a lean-faced, hawk-nosed old lady, whose bright black eyes betrayed that she had more than traveller blood. Her imperious features were framed in a cascade of silver hair, bound across her brow with an embroidered red fillet.

As we entered she gave a gap-toothed grin and raised her wrinkled and bejewelled hands. 'Mr Tyroll, young lady,' she welcomed us. 'Come in and have a seat,' and she dismissed Paddy with a wave.

We sat alongside her and as our eyes grew accustomed to the colourful gloom of the trailer I realised that a tall, silent girl stood behind the rocking-chair. She now turned it to face us and vanished into the rear of the trailer.

Queenie leaned forward, her jewellery throwing sparkles in our faces. She took my left hand and Sheila's right in hers and held them side by side. She looked up, gazing from one to another of us.

'Paddy Murphy says you have troubles,' she stated, 'but there are no troubles so bad they will not end. You have been a help to me and mine in trouble, Mr Tyroll, now I must help you and your lady.'

She brushed our palms with the side of her old, dry thumbs. 'I am traveller and Romany,' she said, 'I have the *kohli rat*, the black blood of India. I can see and I can tell.'

She fell silent, hunched over our hands. When she spoke again her voice was quieter, more sing-song.

'Love and danger,' she said, 'love and danger. Here is love, true love that you must not deny, but you must not stay together for the danger. You are made for each other, it is in your blood. You have the blood of all the world in you and the lady has the travelling blood. She has come a long way to find you and you have waited a long time for her, but you are one and shall be one.'

She paused again and lifted her piercing eyes to our faces, but she seemed to be looking through us and beyond. Then she began again.

'You do not know what it is you know, but there are evil men who seek you. You must go back, go back to Belston where the answer is, but the lady must not go. There is great danger there for her; she must stay among us. Her people were miners and some were travellers. She should be with her people where we can protect her. There is an old man in her heart, a tall, brave old man who is gone. You are sad and angry for his death, my dear, but you must hide now.

'You,' she said to me, 'must go back, but do not go home. Those who seek you have placed a thing in your home that will trap you. It will trap you with this very hand. Do not go near it, it will do you harm. There is a picture in your heads, an old picture that you do not understand. Look into the picture. What you must know is all there. Look into the picture.'

Her voice trailed away and she clasped both of our hands together in hers.

'Such love,' she said, 'such love, and dangers that will pass, but do not go home, Mr Tyroll, do not go home.'

She relinquished our hands and looked up again, smiling her almost toothless smile. She called her attendant who hurried out of the rear of the trailer with tall glasses of beer and we all drank in silence.

When the glasses were empty she looked at us, her head on one side. 'Did I tell you the truth, Mr Tyroll?'

'I do believe you did,' I said. 'It agrees with what I was thinking.'

114

'I can see and I can tell,' she repeated. 'Then go and do what you must,' she commanded, 'and leave your lovely lady with us. I shall protect her till you come.'

Moments later, when we stood outside the trailer, Sheila blinked in the morning sun.

'Phew!' she exclaimed. 'Is that old identity for real?'

'Very real,' I said. 'I've seen her do that a dozen times and she seems to know.'

'But she could have got all that stuff from Paddy, couldn't she?'

'Not about your mining ancestors, she couldn't,' I said.

'What did she mean that you have the blood of all the world?'

'I've never told her, but my grandfather was a circus performer, from generations of them. She's probably right. I do have the blood of all the world and I bet there's a drop of Romany blood somewhere.'

'You're full of surprises, aren't you, Chris Tyroll?' she said. 'She knew about that. What was the bit about the coaly rat or whatever?'

'That's Romany,' I said, 'the gypsy language. It means "black blood", the pure old dark-skinned Romany blood from northern India. Those who have it are very proud of it. Old Queenie is what the Roms call a *diddikoi*.'

'I thought that was just a gypsy?'

'No. Only settled people think it means that. It's a Romany word that means a half-breed gypsy-traveller.'

'Well, what's the difference between travellers and gypsies?'

'I told you – the travellers have been here since God knows when, some say the Bronze Age. They have a language called Shelta. It's a jumble of words from all over but the bedrock of it is one of the oldest tongues in Europe. The Romany gypsies came here five hundred years ago, from India. Their language is Romany which is a dialect of Sanskrit.'

'My oath!' she exclaimed. 'How can you tell them apart?'

I laughed. 'There's only supposed to be one way. Gypsies think that roasted hedgehog is a delicacy; travellers think that eating hedgehogs is a dirty habit.'

'What's a hedgehog?' she asked, and I had to start explaining all over again.

At lunchtime Paddy brought Miley to the trailer. 'He'll see you to Shrewsbury,' he said, jerking his thumb at the gangling, blond youth, 'and you see that he drives you safely.'

Sheila clung to me before we left. 'Be careful!' she commanded. 'Remember what Queenie said about a trap.'

'I've never been daft enough to ignore one of Queenie's warnings,' I said. 'I guess she means that the enemy's bugged my house.'

'Maybe,' she said, 'but they're killers. They might have booby-trapped it with one of their damned firebombs. Just look after yourself, Chris Tyroll.'

Miley and I left in mid-afternoon. Even to my non-expert eyes I could see that the lad's latest car was a low, open-topped early sixties job, older than me, but once we were under way it was soon apparent that it had a lot more power than it needed. We dropped down across the dam road and, in minutes, the little cluster of trailers was out of sight.

At the first small town we came to I got Miley to stop, so that I could buy a jacket, a shirt and a few other necessaries. Coming out of the little gents' outfitters I was dismayed to find a presence of uniformed security men in the street, and had to remind myself that all their uniforms looked alike; this team were evidently collecting a payroll from the bank.

Half an hour later Miley said, 'Look in the mirror.'

I looked. Well back behind us was a dark green van, the same colour as the security van that had stood outside the bank.

'Is he following?' I asked.

'I think so. Watch this.'

Miley swung us off the main road into a left turning and followed a winding lane up a hillside. From the brow we could see that the van had turned off after us.

'He's not going anywhere that we're not,' said Miley.

'They must have spotted me at the shops back there,' I said. 'What do we do now?'

'Get rid of him, that's what!'

19

Miley drove steadily for a short time, until the van dropped from sight behind us, then he slammed his foot to the floor and the car leapt away beneath us. I grabbed the door-top and hung on for dear life as he twisted the vehicle through the narrow road, flinging it into amazing turns around rocky outcrops and through deep gullies.

At last we turned the corner of a rocky bluff and came out on a stretch of open moorland, dotted with rocks, across which the road wound. The car jolted across an iron cattle-grid and, beyond it, Miley stamped on the brake, almost hurling me through the windscreen. Before I had recovered he had sprung from the car and was racing back along the road, shouting, 'Come on! Come on!'

I dived out and ran after him, catching him up by the cattle-grid. He was stooped over one end, trying to lift it from over the concrete-lined pit that it covered.

'Get the other end!' he commanded. 'Let's have it off!'

I followed his order and began to lift at my end, but I protested when I realised what he had in mind. 'You can't do it!' I said. 'You'll kill him!'

'Ah, not at all,' he panted. 'He'll have a seat-belt. He'll just get a few bruises.'

Together we succeeded in dragging the iron grid from its setting of impacted dirt. With a joint heave we turned it over like a big lid and dropped it on the nearside of the pit. As it clanged on to the road surface Miley sprinted for the car and I followed.

We tumbled in and he roared away across the moor, suddenly reversing on to the grass and pulling behind a jumble of rocks. Snatching something from the glove compartment, he leapt out again and slid quickly along the side of the rocks, until he could see the cattle-grid without being seen. I hunched behind him and realised that he had taken a pair of expensive binoculars from the car.

We could hear the approaching note of the van's engine and I tensed, still fearing that I was about to become an accomplice to murder. The van suddenly appeared around the rocky bluff beyond the grid.

The driver had no chance. If he even had time to realise what was in front of him, he had no time to do anything about it. The vehicle's nose plunged into the pit with a reverberating crash, the rear end lifted until the van was almost vertical, then settled on to the far side of the pit with a thud that shook the ground.

I half rose, intending to go and see what damage had been done, but Miley pushed me down with one hand. After a silence broken only by hissing from the wrecked engine of the canted van, bangs began to echo from the wreck and the driver's door opened slowly. A uniformed figure clambered stiffly out and sat on the edge of the pit. I released the breath I had been holding since the van appeared.

Miley lifted the glasses. 'Look at that!' he said after a moment, and passed me the glasses. 'I told you they wasn't wobs after you. Look at his badges!'

I focused the binoculars and scanned the driver. The uniform was a close imitation of police style, but not the badge on the shoulder. A pale green flash with silver initials leapt into my view – KES. I had seen that flash often in and around Belston and well knew what it signified – Kerrenwood Enterprises Security. So Kerrenwood's were backing up the enemy.

I had no time to think about why Kerrenwood's were involved. Miley snatched the glasses back and made for the car. Seconds later he swung out on to the road and we were away across the moor. A mile further on we reached the far side of the hill, where the road began a zigzagging descent among rocks, as steep as the way we had climbed on the other slope. Below us lay a broad open valley, through which a road ran like a ruled line towards distant hills.

'A Roman road,' I said.

'So 'tis,' said Miley, 'and the only way from here to Shrewsbury which might be troublesome.'

'Why's that?'

'Because the queer fella behind us had a radio aerial on his
van. If his radio's still working he'll be calling up more of the
same and they'll know where we're going. All they'll do is sit
in those hills and wait for us.'

I looked across the landscape. The afternoon had dulled and
the sky was unbroken grey, but it was possible to see what he
meant. We had burned a bridge behind us and must drop
down to the straight road and follow it into the border hills.

'Then don't take me to Shrewsbury,' I said. 'You can't take
me into the town by car, anyway. We'll be sitting ducks in that
traffic spiral if they're waiting for us there.'

'I told you,' he said, 'they'll wait for us in the hills. They're
not going to be murdering people in town.'

'Then turn aside and drop me somewhere,' I said. 'I can find
my way to Shrewsbury or get a ride through to the Midlands
or whatever.'

'Me daddy said I was to get you safe to the train at
Shrewsbury,' he said, stubbornly, 'and he's a great old one for
doing things right, is me daddy.'

He navigated us down to the road and turned right on to it,
beginning to build up speed as soon as he had the long straight
in front of him. I was silent, knowing I had lost the argument,
but he returned to it.

'Look at that,' he said, indicating the hills ahead. I followed
his gesture and saw that a curtain of rain was falling between
us and the hills.

'I couldn't drop you in that,' he said. 'You'd be drenched and
me daddy would never forgive me.'

Now I was sure there was no alternative plan, but I didn't
fancy a confrontation somewhere in those rainswept hills with
the sports-jacketed killer and his thugs. Even if, by a miracle,
we evaded that, there was the prospect of being simply surrounded on the pavement in Shrewsbury.

The curtain of rain moved steadily out from the hills to meet us, until Miley had to stop and drag up a battered hood to keep out the worst of it. Now we were disadvantaged by the reduced visibility. The approaching hills were almost lost to sight behind the drizzle. Miley began to mutter to himself and slow down, driving hunched forward over the wheel and peering intently through the murk.

Suddenly he bumped off the road on to the grass verge and pulled to a stop. Taking the binoculars, he humped his jacket over the back of his head and slid out of the car. I followed suit as he made for the stone wall alongside the road. He climbed across the ditch and perched himself gingerly against the wall, lifting the glasses and trying, with the other hand, to shield the lenses from the rain.

'What are you looking for?' I asked.

'What am I looking at,' he said, and passed the field-glasses, pointing me along the inside of the wall. I couldn't find it in the lens at first. I was sweeping across rainswept grass. Then suddenly it was there – the rear of a dark green van parked in a field gateway.

We slid back into the comparatively dry car. 'A watcher,' I said, 'to radio ahead when we pass by.'

'That'll be it,' he said and started the car.

He turned in the road and accelerated back along our track, making one of his dramatic turns into a gateway on our left. It was a farm access and we bumped and slithered along a rutted and muddy track towards a cluster of stone buildings at the foot of a steep hill.

'We can't hide up here!' I exclaimed. 'They'll track us here soon and God knows what they'll do to anyone who hides us!'

He never replied, but drove on until the track passed between two buildings and brought us into the yard of the farm. An elderly man, presumably alerted by the sound of our engine, stepped out from the side of an open stone barn as though to greet us. Miley ignored him and drove on between the barn and what was obviously the farmhouse. The track led on to a flimsy wooden gate.

He rubbed the corroded St Christopher medallion pinned on

120

the dash and grinned at me. 'Pop out and fix the gate for me,' he said. 'I don't want to let the old fella's sheep and cows get all over.'

We slid to a halt at the gate. As I jumped out I heard shouts from the old man who was stumbling down the track behind us. Long before he could catch up we were through, the gate was closed and Miley was bumping and zigzagging across rough pasture. Then it dawned on me why he had sought the saint's aid. He was going to try and take us over a small mountain without even a dirt-track to assist.

I looked at the dark, wet slope of grass and rock rising in front of us. I couldn't even see it clearly for the rain, but the nearer it got I still couldn't distinguish anything that looked like more than narrow, winding sheep trails on its surface and they weren't wide enough to hold one tyre. It was my turn to give the battered St Christopher medallion a rub. After all, if I've got a patron saint it must be him.

'Miley – ' I began.

'Shut up, Mr Tyroll, and hold on,' he said, without turning his head. 'This is going to be a bit difficult.'

I lowered my head, not to pray because even in my liberal religion I don't believe the Lord encourages folly, but to try and get rid of the picture in front of me. It didn't work; it was in my head as well. And it was changing. We were slipping suddenly sideways to zigzag helplessly till we struck a rock and rolled over on to the soft top – we were shooting upwards across a patch of wet rock and sliding into an uncontrollable spin that sent us cartwheeling to the bottom – we were performing a dozen more failed manoeuvres, each of which ended disastrously and several in the livid orange fire-burst of a TV movie – we were . . .

We were beginning to lurch upwards. The horrors in my head vanished and I looked up. All I could see was the thin, slick covering of grass stretching upwards to patches of rock.

'Lean this way,' commanded Miley. 'Put your arm around me and lean right over.'

I slid my right arm around his thin, hard shoulders and

121

pressed against him, trying desperately not to interfere with his control of the vehicle. At any moment I expected his foot to go down and the disaster to begin.

I was wrong. With our weight as far to the driver's side as he could get it, he had inched the wheels on that side on to the bottom of a sheep trail. Now he edged forward slowly, his feet working like a cyclist's, his lean, strong hands alternately coaxing and forcing the bucking steering wheel. I glanced at his face and saw a wild, jaw-gritted grin fixed below the boy's blue-grey eyes. They were everywhere at once, on the perilously narrow, muddy track that gave us our only grip on the hillside, on the changing slope ahead of us, on the mirrors and sometimes dead ahead as some new hazard loomed.

Slowly I let out my pent-up breath. Gradually the astonishing skill of my companion became the entire focus of my attention. I forgot that one wrong move of eye, foot or hand could bring us to a crushed or flaming end and bent all my mind to willing him into the right moves though I had no idea what they were until he made them.

How long it went on I couldn't say. Maybe twenty minutes, but it seemed far, far longer. The engine snarled and coughed, the windscreen wipers whined and time vanished. Nearly half-way up the slope our ribbon of track bent across the top of a patch of rock. Suddenly the wheels' grip gave way and we were sliding left.

Fighting the wheel with his right hand, Miley reached out with his left and jerked me further towards him, leaning right forward so that I was sprawled between his back and the driver's seat. 'I told you it was difficult!' he muttered.

The sickening slither stopped and gradually he inched the wheels round, seeking an inch of purchase on the bare, wet rock where even mountain sheep would not trust their feet. We found it and we crept upwards again for a few more minutes.

Then the engine stopped and we came to rest. 'You can sit up now, Mr Tyroll,' he said.

Cautiously I levered myself back into my own seat and peered around. We were two-thirds of the way up and on the left shoulder of the hill. Generations of sheep had rounded the hillside here, their feet wearing a platform in the hillside, and there we sat with a view into the valley beyond.

I breathed long and deeply and felt my sweat-sodden shirt cooling on me. I gave my friend Christopher a grateful pat. 'Have you got a fag to spare?' asked Miley.

We smoked silently for several minutes, then I said, 'What next?'

'Down there,' he replied. Two hundred yards below us a narrow lane crossed the hillside and wound down into the valley to join the road we had abandoned miles back.

Miley flung his cigarette end out of the window and started the engine. 'Lean back,' he said, 'it's still a bit steep.'

So it was, but it was ease itself compared to the way up. The only difficult bit came as we neared the little road, cut off from the hillside by a sharper slope and a hawthorn hedge. Miley dealt with the problem by a long, accelerated slant across the slope, taking out about twenty-five yards of hedge as we angled through it and jolted down on to the tarmac, covered in enough hawthorn sprays to camouflage us.

Again he begged a cigarette and we took a rest. Behind us along the valley a train hooter sounded and he looked out. 'Here we go!' he said and we rocketed away in his old style, bounding and slithering through the winding lane until we reached a crossroads at the valley bottom. His driving had long since ceased to bother me. So far as I was concerned, Miles Murphy could take a car to the moon if the fancy took him and I'd be happy to go along.

At the crossroads he surprised me by following our lane across the road into its unsignposted continuation. A few twists and turns later a loud bell rang ahead and we came round a corner in time to see the bar of a level crossing dropping across the road. To our right lay a small country rail station.

Miley braked sharply in front of the bar. 'There it is,' he said. 'Your train to Shrewsbury's coming in. Don't get off the station there. They'll be looking for you outside.'

I scrambled out of the car, dragging the bag that contained my few purchases. 'Miley,' I gasped, 'you're a marvel!'

He grinned his toothy grin. 'I'm a fair ould driver,' he said, 'but me daddy'll skelp me for not driving you to Shrewsbury, so he will. Now get on that train, Mr Tyroll, else he'll kill me dead!'

I ducked under the bar and jogged along the trackside, climbing the steps on to the little platform just as the two-carriage train shuddered to a halt. Minutes later I was seated in the rear carriage as the little train pulled out. Miley gave me a cheery wave as we crossed in front of him.

The train's even rhythm made me feel quite queasy after the jolting, lurching and zooming of the last couple of hours, and the fat Welsh conductor eyed my dishevelled appearance disapprovingly as he issued my ticket.

'Cut it a bit fine, didn't you?' he remarked.

'Yes,' I said, 'we had a bit of trouble on the road.'

20

Shrewsbury station was quiet. I had forty-five minutes before the Wolverhampton train, so I settled down in the snack bar to try and ease my unsettled stomach. It wasn't the train's motion, it was a flood of adrenalin washing about with no immediate emergencies to make it useful.

I was settled in a corner, hidden behind somebody else's forgotten newspaper, when I heard a loud Brummy voice at the counter asking for a tray of six coffees to take out. A cautious glance around the newspaper's pages revealed a tall man in KES uniform who was chatting up the attendant as she filled his order. Miley had been right. They had the outside of the station well covered. I drew back behind my paper and when he left he was far too busy not spilling his mates' refreshments to pay any attention to an *Independent* reader in the corner.

Twenty minutes later I was rattling away to Wolverhampton, humming 'Ye banks and braes' – you know, the bit about 'You tak' the high road and I'll tak' the low road'. It hadn't been the best day of my life, but it was turning out a lot better than it might have done.

I spent the night in a commercial hotel on the edge of Wolverhampton, calling my articled clerk, Alan Reilly, at home to pick me up in Wolves the next morning. Before nine next day Alan and I were letting ourselves in at the back door of the office. While he went to fix the coffee, I heard two cars pull into the yard and a moment later Claude and my assistant, Alasdair Thayne, let themselves in.

Claude the Phantom is ex-Services Investigation and looks it. Over six foot, broad-built, with a round, fair face and close-cropped greying hair, he always dresses in an anonymous grey suit and razor-starched white shirts that would advertise detergents. Sometimes the appearance is against him. I once sent him to interview some hippy witnesses in a Nottingham drugs case. He'd been gone two hours when I got a phone call complaining that an obvious CID officer was in Nottingham pretending to be my enquiry agent. On the other hand, he happens to be the best.

Alasdair Thayne is a very different kettle of fish. Shropshire born of an old county family, public school and Oxford educated, first class law degree, he should have been lolling behind an antique desk in London, pulling five hundred quid an hour for helping City crooks launder money. He'd been with me two years, since he answered an ad in *Private Eye* when I finally decided that I needed an assistant. When I saw this tall, elegant young man, with a posh drawl, slicked-back hair, a pencil moustache and tailored suits that all created a kind of twenties atmosphere, I couldn't imagine what he wanted with my practice.

'I rather thought it might be a bit more interesting than drawing wills and conveyances and helping unsavoury chappies evade tax, Mr Tyroll,' he explained. I think that was the last time he called me 'Mr Tyroll'. Since then it's always been 'governor' or 'boss'. I bet he calls his father 'pater'.

I had misgivings about employing him, but I didn't have options. In three interviews two candidates turned me down before the interviews ended, so Alasdair won by default. Lucky chance, because he turned out to have a brilliant brain and an absolutely imperturbable manner in crises. In courts his coolness convinces magistrates that the most unlikely stories are true, and little old ladies and hardened Black Country villains think the world of him.

He lounged into a chair while Claude went to help Alan with the coffee. He pulled a battered tin from his pocket and began rolling a cigarette. He ought to smoke Sullivans or Freibourg and Treyer to support his image, but he rolls evil-smelling things out of foreign tobaccos which he buys in a back-street shop. I suppose it's the only way he can afford his suits on the wages I pay him.

When the product was fuming well and scattering smouldering debris on to the edge of my desk, he asked, 'Did you get to see the unused documents in Gormley's case, governor?'

'Yes and no,' I said. 'Inspector Saffary showed me anything that wouldn't help and flatly refused to show me the radio log and the incident log.'

'Why did you think they'll help?'

'Look, Karen Worstance was raped at nine in the evening of a Thursday. Gormley was breathalysed and taken to the nick at midnight on Saturday. While he was being processed for the breathalyser affair, Saffary hooked him and questioned him about the rape. Why? My information is that until that amazing hunch of Saffary's, the entire division had been looking for a man who looked nothing like Gormley. I wanted to confirm that and find out what made Saffary question Gormley.'

'But he did confess on tape, boss.'

'And withdrew that confession to us. You know Gormley, he's ten per cent subnormal and he tries to please people, to tell them what they want to hear. And you know Saffary – he's a hard-faced, beady-eyed pig, who exudes the threat of violence without moving or speaking!'

He drew hard on his smouldering construction. 'So where next?'

'Superintendent Howard has backed Saffary's refusal. We can apply to the court if necessary or we can risk putting Miss

Worstance in the box at the committal and go for her identification.'

'That,' he said slowly, 'would require a bit of thinking about.'

'So think about it, Alasdair. We'll talk about it in a couple of days.'

Alan and Claude returned with a tray of coffee. A moment later the front door rattled and Jayne looked around the door of my room. Her black eyes widened at the sight of the four of us.

'Good morning!' she said. 'Wet your beds, boys, or have you been partying all night?'

'As a matter of fact,' I said, 'we've been drafting an application to the EU for a grant for voice-operated word-processors, so we can save on two typists' salaries.'

'Humph!' she said. 'They won't make the coffee, polish your desk and sort out clients you've upset.'

'Alan,' I commanded, 'make the lady a coffee. Jayne, fetch six shorthand notebooks and a box of pencils. I've got a long job to dictate.'

'Wouldn't it be better to put it on tape?'

'No,' I said, 'I want everyone to hear and comment as I go, including you.' Another reason was that I hadn't worked out yet how I was going to break the news to her that I'd let a bunch of thugs firebomb her auntie's legacy. It might go better with witnesses present.

We settled again, and I began dictating a complete account of the whole affair, starting with my original dealings with Walter Brown. Occasionally Alasdair or Claude would inject a question for clarification, but basically things proceeded fairly smoothly.

I came to Saturday night, glossing over the intimate details but still provoking covert smirks and knowing glances among my audience. I began to slow down as I drew towards the firebombing. Jayne, head down, was still scribbling industriously.

I couldn't dodge it any longer. As baldly as possible I narrated our evacuation of the cottage and what followed. When I described the twin fireballs that had consumed the

127

bungalow, Jayne's pencil stopped and she jerked her head up, white-faced and wide-eyed.

'Good Lord!' she exclaimed. 'Is Sheila all right?'

I could have kissed her for that reaction, but it was taking all my courage to look her in the eye.

'So far as I know,' I said, 'Sheila is very well, but I'm afraid your cottage is a heap of ash.'

She waved her pencil dismissively. 'That's all right,' she said, 'it was fully insured. They will pay out for arson by government agents, won't they?'

'I guess', I said, 'that in a day or two the Welsh police will officially inform you that your holiday retreat has been burned by the Sons of Glendower.'

'Who are they?'

'The Welsh protestors who burn English-owned cottages in Wales. I have a feeling they're going to carry the can for this one, so there shouldn't be any insurance problems.'

'Well,' she said brightly. 'I never liked the layout. I can change it when it's redone, can't I?'

'Yes,' I said, gratefully. 'If there's any excess expense problem, Jayne, I'll meet it.'

She gave me one of her expressionless stares. 'Out of all those legal aid fees the Board withholds when its budget runs low?' she said. 'Well, ah!' and she bent her head again and set pencil to paper to show the topic was closed.

I went on to the end, leaving out only Sheila's wild proposal and my stunned acceptance. They'd know if that came to pass. When I signified that I'd done, Jayne left to begin typing a small book. The other three sat staring at me.

'Doesn't look much like James Bond,' Claude remarked to Alasdair.

'Hidden depths, old boy, hidden depths,' said Alasdair.

'Lovely manners, though,' said Claude. 'Takes the Aussie lady off for a dirty weekend in Wales, gets her firebombed, half drowned and shot at, leaves her with a pack of tinkers, but still calls her "doctor". You'd think they hadn't been introduced.'

'All right,' I said. 'Keep the bad jokes. I made you listen to all

128

that because I'm a target, Dr McKenna's a target and since we don't know why, you'd better behave as if any associate of this office is on the list. Walk carefully and avoid dark alleys and strangers.'

They nodded, sobered. I took advantage of the change of mood. 'Now,' I said, 'let's try and make a bit of money. What court appointments have we got this week?'

Alasdair reached for my desk diary. In the instant before he touched it, the morning sun slanting through the windows shone across its shiny plastic binding, and in that instant I saw the teeth of the trap that Queenie had foretold. I slapped his outstretched hand away and pushed the diary away from him.

He recoiled, startled. 'Don't touch it!' I snapped. 'Alan, Alasdair, you can go. Claude, I need your services immediately and a bunch of trustworthy experts. I think I know what the bastards have done!'

The two Als left the room, casting bemused glances back-wards. Quickly I briefed Claude on what I needed him to do and what other experts he should involve. All the time the sun crept across my desk, clearly revealing to me that on the back cover of my desk diary were four small rectangular marks, spread in an arc across the lower right-hand corner.

By lunchtime Claude had gone about his business and at last I could get to mine. I felt greatly relieved now I thought I knew what to expect, and got through a lot of routine work.

I never left the office without Alan Reilly alongside for days. I took a room at the Victoria and each evening my phone arrangements with Sheila worked. We had quick, anonymous chats. She told me that Paddy had broken camp and they were moving day by day. I warned her not to tell me where she was. Each call made me miss her more, but she was still safer where she was.

I dined with Alasdair at the Victoria each night. He improved my knowledge of wines enormously. On the night after our office conference, Claude joined us and presented his reports. Alasdair advised on a good celebration bottle when he saw my mood, though he didn't know what the reports said. I knew that I was ready for the next round of the game. For once I understood what the attack was and where it would come from and I was ready. I gave them a toast.

'To Queenie Connors!' I declared. 'May the good Lord give her another ninety years!'

They laughed and drank and Claude smiled knowingly at me.

The attack came a few mornings later. I had not long arrived in the office when Jayne put her head round my door.

'There's two police officers in reception,' she said. 'They say they must speak to you personally.'

I picked up the intercom. 'Alasdair,' I said, 'bring the file I gave you and come to my room. We've got visitors.'

'Show them in,' I told Jayne, and she was back in a moment, ushering them in.

It was Howard, looking grimmer than usual, and Saffary, the bull-necked Ulster sadist. He and I were old enemies. He suffered from fundamentalist beliefs – that all suspects were guilty and that all defence lawyers were pinko crooks. Now he stood half a pace behind his boss, looking for all the world like a well-dressed toad with curly greying hair. He was having difficulty concealing a smirk.

I waved them to chairs, but they remained standing.

'Mr Tyroll,' said Howard, 'I am Detective Superintendent Howard and this is Detective Inspector Saffary from Belston police station. We are here to arrest you on suspicion of offences against the Theft Act and the Official Secrets Act and of the common law offence of attempting to pervert the course of justice. I have to warn you that you need not say anything, but it may harm your defence if you fail to mention anything which you later rely on in court. Anything you do say may be given in evidence.'

Saffary's smile broadened. Alasdair stepped into the open doorway, his briefcase in his hand. I stood up.

'Very well,' I told Howard. 'Alasdair, these officers have arrested me. Please accompany me to the police station as my representative.'

'Absolutely, governor,' he said, apparently unruffled.

Howard grimaced. 'Mr Tyroll, in the circumstances of this particular case it might not be appropriate for a member of your own office to represent you. Mr Thayne might have to be called as a witness.'

'So he might,' I agreed, 'but the choice of solicitor is mine, unless you are prepared to state that Mr Thayne is an unsuitable person to attend me.'

His small mouth tightened and he shook his head.

'Right,' I said. 'Let's go!'

'Before we leave,' he said, 'there is one further matter. Do you consent to a search of your home?'

'Of course,' I said affably. I took out my keys and detached a front door key, handing it to him.

'Now shall we go?' I said.

21

The light above the video-camera in Interview Room One glowed steadily. Howard cleared his throat and began the ritual introduction, reciting for the microphone's benefit the date and time and the fact that this interview was being recorded in Video Interview Room Number One at Belston police station.

After arriving and going through the custody officer's form-filling I had been placed in a cell, where Alasdair sat and drummed on his briefcase. After a bit I pleaded with him to roll one of his disgusting cigarettes.

'Do you want one?' he asked, surprised.

'No,' I said, 'but this place smells of old sweat, the chemicals they wipe the plastic mattresses down with and hopelessness, and I'm not feeling hopeless.'

He rolled one, lit it and sat drumming his fingers and smoking. At one point he asked, 'What are they waiting for, boss?'

'They're not going to start the interview till Howard knows the search team is on its way back.'

He nodded and silence fell again. Minutes later we were invited to the interview room.

'This interview is being conducted by me, Superintendent Howard of Central Midlands CID. Also present are . . .' and he trailed off for us to introduce ourselves.

'Detective Inspector Saffary, Central Midlands CID,' announced the Ulsterman.

'Alasdair Thayne, assistant solicitor, Tyrolls, Belston,' drawled my assistant and Howard nodded at me.

'Christopher Tyroll, sole partner in Tyrolls, present as unwilling detainee to whom no proper explanation of his arrest has yet been made.'

Saffary glowered behind his spectacles and Howard pursed his mouth.

When I had made my statement Howard cleared his throat and started again.

'In view of your remark, Mr Tyroll, I am stating now that you have been arrested on suspicion of possible offences against the Official Secrets Act and the Theft Act and on suspicion of the common law offence of attempting to pervert the course of justice.'

I opened my mouth, but he raised a hand to forestall me and carried on.

'I have to tell you that you have been arrested and your continued detention authorised in order to obtain evidence by questioning. You do not have to say anything, but if you fail to mention any fact on which you later seek to rely in your defence the court's attention may be drawn to your failure to mention it. Anything you do say may be taken down and given in evidence. Do you understand?'

'I am still dissatisfied with your explanation of my arrest but I understand the caution. In essence you mean that silence on any point may be interpreted by a court as evidence of guilt.'

'I am not here to argue legal interpretation with you, Mr Tyroll,' declared Howard. 'This interview is to obtain evidence

132

by questioning and I believe you will find that, as the questions progress, any doubts you have as to the nature of my enquiries will be cleared up.'

He opened the folder on the table in front of him and scanned a manuscript document. I could see that it was in the tight, mechanically neat script of Inspector Saffary.

'Now, Mr Tyroll,' Howard began again, 'do you agree that on Tuesday 14th May this year you telephoned Detective Inspector Saffary at this police station and had a conversation with him about a client of yours called Darren Gormley?'

'Yes,' I replied. 'Your control room tape-recorder will have recorded the call.' They hate you knowing that they tape all incoming calls.

'I have no idea what you mean about tape-recording,' he said. 'Do you agree that, in the course of that conversation, you requested access to various documents in police custody of which copies had not been supplied to you?'

'Yes.'

He nodded. 'And can you further confirm that an appointment was made for you to meet with Detective Inspector Saffary at this police station the following afternoon in order to examine those documents?'

'Yes.'

'Is it true that, at 3.10 p.m. on the following afternoon, you kept that appointment here and that, in the CID office of this station, Detective Inspector Saffary produced to you two boxes of documents relating to Gormley's case?'

'No.'

Both of them blinked.

I went on to explain. 'Inspector Saffary had two boxes of documents in his possession. So far from producing both boxes to me, he insisted that I ask for specific items and then, with the exception of one item, produced the specific document requested to me. I have no way of knowing what fraction or percentage I saw of the documents contained in the two boxes, but I believe it to have been very little.'

Saffary's eyes narrowed behind his spectacles, but Howard

went on smoothly. 'Do you agree that among the documents that you requested sight of was the incident log and the radio messages log relating to the incident?'

'Yes, but I was not shown them.'

'Why was that?'

'Because Inspector Saffary informed me that so far as he was concerned I had no legitimate reason to see those documents and that, under the powers of the Criminal Investigations and Procedure Act 1996, he was refusing me a sight of them.' If you don't know about that Act, it's the one they passed after years of the Court of Appeal telling the Crown Prosecution Service that it must make full disclosure of evidence to prevent little problems like the Birmingham Six case or the Bridgwater Three or any of those. It says that it's up to the police to decide what gets disclosed to the defence, so there. It should keep the Court of Appeal busy for the next twenty-five years.

'Did you at any time see the folder containing those documents?'

'When I first made my request to see the documents, I recall that Inspector Saffary looked in one of the boxes and lifted out a dark blue ring-binder with the Central Midlands badge embossed on it. He told me that it contained those documents, but since I never saw the contents I have no idea whether he told me the truth or not.'

Saffary grunted contemptuously. Howard glanced at him and then returned to me. 'So you never at any time handled that folder containing the incident log and radio log while at this police station?'

'I never at any time handled the dark blue folder which the inspector said contained those documents.'

'What did you do when Detective Inspector Saffary refused to show you the documents that you had requested?'

'I asked him to refer the matter to you for a decision.'

'Did you give any explanation of your desire to have access to those particular documents?'

Alasdair intervened quickly. 'I have to advise Mr Tyroll not to answer that question,' he drawled smoothly, 'on the basis that any answer may reveal matter confidential to the defence of Mr Tyroll's client, Darren Gormley, and that the question is thereby an improper one.'

I smiled. 'Thank you, Alasdair,' I said, 'but the fact is I gave Inspector Saffary a complete explanation of my reasons. I have no doubt that my reasons are recorded in Inspector Saffary's memorandum in front of you, but for the record I told him that I was aware that for forty-eight hours after the rape of Karen Worstance enquiries had been pursued about a suspect whose physical description was totally different from that of my client. It was only after Darren Gormley was arrested for a breath-alyser matter and brought to this police station that Inspector Saffary decided to question him in connection with the rape.'

Saffary leaned forward. 'Are you implying', he asked, ponderously, 'that I set out to frame your client Gormley?'

I eyed him steadily because I knew he hated it. In interrogations he liked to deploy the considerably offensive power of his own nasty eyes, not to be outstared by suspects. 'I am stating, not implying, Inspector, that I found the circumstances under which Darren Gormley came to be charged with rape so unusual as to arouse a suspicion that something abnormal had taken place. Only you know whether that suspicion is correct. Would you like to tell me now, for the record, the reasons why you began to question Gormley?'

His face flushed and the eyes bulged. 'You are here to answer questions, not to ask them!' he snarled.

'Precisely,' cut in Howard. 'Mr Tyroll, what happened when you asked Detective Inspector Saffary to consult me for a further opinion?'

'He left the CID office, apparently to telephone you. There being about half a dozen phones in the room we were in, I imagine he wanted to offer you opinions of me that he was not prepared to let me overhear. After a few minutes he returned and stated that you had confirmed that, under the 1996 Act, you were not prepared to give me access to the documents requested.'

'And what happened then?'

'I thanked Mr Saffary for his co-operation and left.'

'And you took no documents with you?'

'No. I had made notes from those few documents that the inspector was prepared to show me.'

'You did not take the radio and incident log folder?'

I feigned surprise. 'Of course not! I've told you – I only saw it briefly when the inspector lifted it out of one of the two boxes.'

'And you did not take advantage of Detective Inspector Saffary's absence from the office to look at the folder?'

'If he thought that was a possibility he would never have left me alone with it. Besides, if I had been stupid enough to do so, he could have walked in on me. He was only gone less than five minutes.'

Howard looked down again at Saffary's memo. 'Are you aware', he asked, 'that police documents not disclosed to the defence are classified as confidential and fall under the provisions of the Official Secrets Act?'

'No,' I said. 'I know of no statutory authority for that proposition, but I do know that what you say is the view taken by police officers.'

Howard turned and looked at Saffary and a flicker that could have been a smile passed across both faces. They were coming to some kind of a crunch.

Howard leaned forward across the table and stared directly at me. 'Let me get this absolutely clear, Mr Tyroll. At no time, according to what you have told us, at no time at all did you ever handle the dark blue folder containing the incident and radio log in Darren Gormley's case. Is that correct?'

'At no time', I repeated, 'did I ever handle the dark blue folder which Mr Saffary told me contained the incident and radio logs relating to my client Darren Gormley.'

The superintendent breathed deeply and leant back from the table. He believed that the hook was firmly inserted.

'I have to tell you', he said, 'that when Detective Inspector Saffary next examined the Gormley documents, during yesterday afternoon, the blue folder was missing from them. The Document Store records show that they had not been out of the store since they were shown to you. Would you care to comment on that situation?'

'No,' I said, 'except to say that the most likely explanation is that Saffary failed to return it to the Document Store or that it has subsequently been improperly removed.'

Saffary was so happy he didn't even glower at the use of his unadorned surname. He was almost smiling. Howard too was becoming more relaxed.

'That', he said, 'is extremely unlikely – virtually impossible. It is a great deal more likely that you, having been refused access to those documents, asked Detective Inspector Saffary to telephone me so that he would leave the office and give you the opportunity to remove the folder in his absence. Is that not what happened?'

At last he had come to his accusation and thought he was about to close the trap. I decided to play along a little longer.

'That is not what happened,' I said. 'Firstly because, as I have already pointed out, there are half a dozen phones in the CID office which he might have used. Secondly because I am not a fool or a thief, and thirdly because I am a solicitor of the Supreme Court, bound by rules of behaviour far stricter than those which regulate the conduct of police officers or the general public.' That sounded sufficiently pompous, so I stopped.

'I note what you say,' he replied, equally pompously. 'Nevertheless, it is my view and that of Detective Inspector Saffary that the most likely explanation is that the folder was taken by you because you had been refused access to the contents. With that in mind, I requested your consent to a search of your home, which you gave me, and that search has been carried out.'

Whether he had some concealed signalling method I don't know, or perhaps the whole stilted performance had been worked to a timetable, but at that moment there was a rap on the interview room door and a young detective constable entered.

'Detective Constable Peters is now entering the interview room,' chanted Howard for the microphone.

The young DC apologised for interrupting and handed Howard a slip. The superintendent smiled again at Saffary and then looked down at the note. The smile vanished and he shoved it along the table to the inspector, keeping his hand across it so that I should not see it. I didn't need to.

Saffary's jowls dropped and his face turned the colour of lard when he saw the note. He stared silently at Howard who rose from his seat and gabbled, 'The time is now 11.45 a.m. and this interview is being interrupted.'

Saffary switched off the camera and followed his boss out of the room, slamming the door. From start to interruption the entire interview had only taken about ten minutes.

'What', said Alasdair, 'was all that in aid of?'

I eased myself in the uncomfortable plastic chair. 'That', I said, 'was an indication that it's dawning on them that they're falling into a hole they dug for me, but don't say too much. The camera lamp's off but that doesn't mean the mike's not operating. You can't trust these bastards as far as you can smell them.'

'Well, we might as well have some refreshment.' Alasdair opened the door and called through to the custody sergeant, 'Any chance of a couple of coffees, sergeant?'

I heard the reply. 'Well, Mr Thayne, the super and Mr Saffary are conferring with the search team so I suppose there'll be time. I'll send some in.'

'Thank you, sergeant,' said Alasdair and pulled his makings tin from his side pocket. 'What do you think they've found?' he asked me.

I nodded at the microphone. 'No doubt Laurel and Hardy will soon be back to tell us,' I said and lit one of my own cigarettes.

Two Styrofoam cups of lukewarm instant coffee were delivered, and we were sipping them when Howard and Saffary returned. They did not look happy.

They seated themselves in silence and, once the equipment was switched on, Howard began the ritual again.

'This interview is now continuing after a break that has lasted until 11.57. The persons present are as before. I must remind you, Mr Tyroll, that you are still under caution. Do you understand?'

'I confirm again that I understand the statutory threat very well.'

'Right,' he said, ignoring the jibe. 'When this interview was interrupted you had confirmed that you had never handled the dark blue folder containing the radio and incident records relating to the arrest of Darren Gormley. Correct?'

'No,' I said. 'I have stated to you, and the videotape will confirm, that I have never handled the folder which your inspector told me contained those records and that I did not remove that folder from the police station. I repeat that I have no means of knowing whether Saffary was telling the truth.'

The inspector snorted and Howard motioned him to be silent. There was a long pause while Howard stared blankly at the folder in front of him. I knew that he had lost his bearings and I decided to go on the offensive.

'May I ask a question, superintendent?'

He looked up. 'You may,' he said shortly.

I leaned forward and sipped at the murky coffee. 'During the break in this interview,' I began, 'the custody sergeant confirmed to Mr Thayne that your search team had returned from my home. Can you save everybody a lot of time by telling me what, if anything, your searchers have found at my house which is of relevance to alleged offences against the Official Secrets Act, the Theft Act, common law offences of conspiracy to pervert the course of justice or any other allegedly criminal matter into which you may be enquiring?'

He turned an uneasy glance at Saffary who shrugged. Howard turned back towards me.

'I can confirm', he began slowly, 'that the search of your home has been completed and that nothing of any relevance to this enquiry has been found.' His eyes and his tone of voice had dropped. Saffary was staring past Alasdair and me at the sound-proofed wall behind us.

'Thank you, superintendent,' I said. 'Now, since I would not have it said at the trial of anyone who is charged with anything arising out of this interview that I was less than co-operative, may I now tell you what I do know about a dark blue folder of documents embossed with the emblem of the Central Midlands Police?'

Saffary's bull-like head swung towards me and Howard's eyes narrowed.

'If you wish,' he said. 'I remind you again that you are still under caution.'

'Thank you,' I said. 'Alasdair, will you please pass me my file?'

It was our turn to bowl.

22

I sipped the gruesome coffee while Alasdair took a fat unmarked file from his briefcase. Howard's and Saffary's eyes never left it as I placed it in front of me and began to take out documents.

'A preliminary question,' I said. 'Having failed to find any evidence of crime at my home, why have you not asked to search my office? Was that because you had reason to suppose that the evidence you expected to find was at my home?'

Saffary heaved forward in his chair and was about to do his 'You're here to answer questions' routine, but Howard stopped him with a hand on his arm. The superintendent, at least, had realised that they hadn't just failed, they were now on very dangerous ground indeed.

'We have not asked to search your office primarily because of the difficulties you would undoubtedly raise about "excepted material" under the Police and Criminal Evidence Act. I do not have to tell you the source of our information, I would only say that we were acting on information received,' said Howard, flatly.

I nodded. 'In that case,' I said, 'I shall begin my explanation.'

'First,' I announced, holding up a sheaf of papers to the camera, 'is a statement by my articled clerk, Mr Alan Reilly, in which he states that he met me at Wolverhampton rail station

140

on my return from a short holiday and took me to my office. It is within his knowledge that I never left the office until he accompanied me to the Victoria Hotel, Belston that evening and saw me register. On the following day, he picked me up from the Victoria Hotel in the morning and is able to state the hours during which I remained at the office before he accompanied me back to the hotel. He picked me up again this morning and is able to state the time at which I arrived at the office. You know the time at which I left.'

'What's the point of all this?' snarled Saffary.

'The point, inspector, is to establish that, since arriving back in Belston, I have never set foot in my home.'

'Reilly's statement won't prove that,' declared the Ulsterman.

'Taken together with other evidence, which will emerge if you stop interrupting, it will. In the meantime, this certified copy of the statement has been made in the Criminal Justice Act format so that it may be readily used in the criminal proceedings which are now almost bound to result from this interview,' and I thrust the copy across the desk at Howard. He took it without glancing at it. His eyes were still fixed on the folder.

'Next,' I continued, holding up another report, 'is a report prepared and signed by Mr Gordon Rains, enquiry agent. I won't bore you with the whole of it, you can study it at your leisure, but let me quote you a few highlights. His report was made subsequent to a request by me to carry out a thorough search of my home,' and I read a part of it aloud:

'"As instructed I attended at the premises in company with Mr Price, a forensic scientist from Brierley Laboratories, Mr Walters, a photographer and Mr Ferry, a security consultant. In accordance with Mr Tyroll's instructions I first carried out a careful survey of the outside of the building. At the rear of the building I discovered that a small pane of glass in a kitchen window had been, apparently, removed and carelessly replaced. The putty surrounding the pane was inexpertly applied and still very soft. There were putty-stained fingerprints on the pane which I asked Mr Walters to photograph, after which Mr Price lifted them with adhesive tape so that they could be examined. Enlarged copies of them are attached to this report." '

I looked up. Howard was sitting back in his chair, white-faced. Saffary's face was flushing rhythmically with dark blotches. For a moment it crossed my mind that I might have the pleasure of seeing him die of apoplexy, but I preferred to see him in the dock of Stafford Crown Court.

I returned to Claude's report. '"A search in the plants close to the kitchen window disclosed a number of fragments of window glass which appeared to have been recently broken. Two of the fragments bore bloodstains. All of them were taken by Mr Price for blood-typing and DNA analysis.

'"Having established that the house had been inexpertly burgled, Mr Ferry and I then entered via the back door and carried out a silent search of the entire premises. In the course of that search I found electronic devices (Mr Ferry describes them as 'VOX micro-transmitters') under the top of the cabinet alongside Mr Tyroll's bed, beneath the top of the coffee table in his sitting-room and underneath the dining-room table. Mr Ferry found similar devices inside the telephone instruments in the bedroom, the sitting-room and the study. As already instructed he neutralised them with devices which he called 'baffle boxes' and left them *in situ*." '

The audience was rapt. I went on:

'"Once the listening devices were neutralised the entire team then carried out a thorough search of the premises. Mr Tyroll had warned me that we might find explosive or incendiary devices, illegal drugs or stolen goods, and that we were to search carefully and safely for anything anomalous. In the event, the only anomalous object which we found was a dark blue plastic-covered file folder embossed with the badge of the Central Midlands Police Force. Having been in the house on many occasions during the last ten years, I am fully aware that Mr Tyroll would never leave case documents in the house while it was unoccupied. Furthermore, the folder was hidden half-way down in a basket of magazines that Mr Tyroll keeps beside his armchair in the sitting-room, a place where he would never leave an important document. I did not touch the folder, but left it to Mr Price to remove it for evidential purposes and carry out any necessary examination."'

I paused again and Saffary almost shouted, 'So you did have the folder at your home! What have you done with it?'

I lobbed Claude's report across at Howard before answering. 'We are in danger of confusing ourselves here,' I said. 'You have heard nothing to suggest that the folder found by Mr Rains was the one allegedly missing from this police station.'

I took out another document. 'This', I said, 'is Mr Price's detailed report. In brief it says that the cover of the dark blue folder found in my home showed signs of having been wiped with a spirit substance and bore what appeared to be the prints of the four fingers of my left hand. However, I'm sure two experienced detectives will know that fingerprints are composed of the oily secretions of the pores of the fingertip and particles of dirt which have clung to it. Chemical and microscopic examination of these prints revealed that they also contained traces of the adhesive used in the clear tape supplied to police forces for lifting fingerprints to be exhibited. Mr Price concludes that the prints are fakes and, having examined the plastic cover of the desk diary in my office, he is satisfied that a genuine set of prints was lifted from the diary with sticky tape and placed on the dark blue folder.'

I shoved the report across at Howard, who continued to say nothing.

'Never mind the forensic rubbish,' said Saffary. 'Where is that folder?'

'Mr Saffary,' interrupted Alasdair, 'surely I don't have to remind an officer of your experience that aggressive and repetitive questioning may well make the record of an interview inadmissible as evidence. I suggest you read *R. v. Malcolm* and *R. v. Abdullahi and Others*.'

Saffary snorted and looked away.

'It's OK, Alasdair,' I said. 'That folder is in the custody of the Document Examination Department at Birmingham University.' I took another report from the file. 'Here is the report of Dr Kanwar on his examination of the folder. Again, I won't bore you with the details, but in essence he says that the documents contained within the folder are forgeries. The radio log was subjected to Electronic Static Deposition analysis which showed that its pages were written at one session and in the wrong order. The faxes in the file, though purporting to come from several different police stations, all bear the same indentification number, which Dr Kanwar says is the number of Whistlehall police station. In other words, gentlemen, the dark blue folder found at my home is not the one allegedly missing from here. It is a stupid forgery.'

I spun that report across the table at Howard and took out the last bundle. 'Here', I said, 'is a set of copies of Mr Walters' photographs, duly certified.' That also went on to the growing heap in front of the superintendent.

I sat back and picked up the cold coffee. 'That, I think, is as far as I can assist you, beyond pointing out that, in addition to my articled clerk's statement, once you trace the tape-recordings made from the illegal bugs in my home you will be able to be quite certain that I have not set foot in the place while this sordid little scam was going on.'

Even Saffary was silent. He had now turned a ripe and unhealthy shade of red. He turned to his pallid, silent superior and looked at him questioningly.

Howard cleared his throat. 'What are you implying by all this?' he said quietly.

'This is not an implication, superintendent. The evidence is clear that, during my absence from my home, it was illegally entered by a burglar of amazing carelessness. Alternatively it may well have been a burglar who thought he was never going to be called to account. The purpose of that entry was to install illegal surveillance equipment and telephone taps and to plant faked evidence in order to secure criminal convictions against me.'

'And why do you believe that this was done?'

'Partly to mislead me as to the true nature of the Gormley investigation, but most importantly to place me in a position where I could no longer cause any embarrassment to the efforts of the police to whitewash the murders of Walter Brown and Francis Cassidy.'

'Why do you implicate police officers in your accusations?'

'At the least because the forged documents were created on genuine police forms and a police fax machine and were contained in a real police folder, and the faked fingerprints showed the chemical constituents of police fingerprint tape.'

His expression never changed. 'Your accusations are very serious,' he said.

I took a two-page photocopy from my file and handed it to him.

'That', I told him, 'is a copy of a letter to the Chief Constable. When I left the office under arrest this morning, my secretary will have carried out my instructions that if I was arrested she was to have copies of all the documents I have given you, together with that letter, sent by courier to the Chief Constable, the Senior Crown Prosecutor at Birmingham and my Member of Parliament. You will see that the letter sets out more detailed allegations of the crimes attempted against me and demands that a full criminal investigation follows. In particular it suggests that the starting point of that investigation should be Detective Inspector Saffary.'

Saffary reared up out of his chair with a strangled exclamation. For once Howard acted swiftly and decisively, thrusting him firmly back into his seat. I was disappointed; I would have loved Saffary to assault me in front of the video-camera.

'Keep your seat, inspector!' Howard snapped. His face was now white – not the pale colour of shock, but the hard white of anger. He had been leaned on to put me out of action and had given the task to Saffary, whose beautifully written memorandum explained how well he'd done it. Now his career was on the line and it had to be Saffary's fault. He stared bleakly at me before speaking again.

'Before I end this interview,' he said, 'would you care to explain why, on returning to Belston, you avoided your home and why you sent Mr Rains and his team to carry out their search?'

I smiled. 'You operated on "information received", superintendent. I had a gypsy's warning, and in case you think that

145

answer is non-responsive, I can assure you that in any trial I am prepared to produce the witness who warned me.'

He looked at me dully, not understanding, then snapped himself back to the official rituals.

'Unless Mr Tyroll wishes to add or clarify anything I propose to end this interview now. Detective Inspector Saffary will give you a form explaining how you can apply for a copy of the video-recording of the interview.'

Saffary pulled open a drawer in the table and thrust a form at me wordlessly. I took it with my brightest smile.

Howard looked at his watch. 'It is now 12.43 p.m. and this interview is ended.'

23

The custody sergeant stood up at his desk as we filed out of the interview room. 'All dealt with according to PACE, superintendent?' he asked Howard.

'The interview has ended and was conducted in accordance with the Police and Criminal Evidence Act, sergeant,' confirmed Howard. 'I now propose to bail Mr Tyroll back to this police station four weeks from today.'

The sergeant pulled a pad of police bail forms towards him. 'Do you consent to bail, Mr Tyroll?' he asked.

'No,' I said. The sergeant looked startled, then smiled faintly. In his long years of service he had probably never heard that reply. 'Then I cannot admit you to bail, Mr Tyroll. You do understand that?'

'I do, sergeant. I also understand that Superintendent Howard must now decide to charge me and bring me rapidly before a court or to release me immediately.'

Howard looked daggers at me. 'Very well,' he said. 'Mr Tyroll is discharged from custody, sergeant,' and he turned on his heel and walked out of the office, closely followed by Saffary.

Minutes later my personal property had been returned, I had signed the Person in Custody Sheet and Alasdair and I were walking across the front lobby of the police station. Saffary's unmistakable voice rang out behind me.

'Mr Tyroll!' he called. 'A moment of your time.'

I turned and waited as he came across to us. 'I should tell you', he said, 'that I have been placed in charge of the Brown and Cassidy enquiries and in that connection I wish to interview your client, Miss McKenna. Where is she?'

'Dr McKenna', I said, emphasising the title, 'is not my client. She is merely the legatee of a former client. She is at present on holiday and I have no idea of her whereabouts. Why do you wish to interview her, inspector? She gave a very full statement to Sergeant Parry.'

His mouth twisted into an unpleasant smirk. 'My review of the file suggests that, as the sole heir of Brown's estate, she had a motive for doing away with him. I propose to examine that aspect of the matter.'

'I suggest', I said, 'that you examine the airline records of flights from Brussels on the day of Walter Brown's death. You'll find her on one of the passenger manifests. She was not even in the country when her grandfather died.'

'That does not mean she was not involved, Tyroll,' he said. 'I intend to interview that young woman.'

'Then if she contacts me I shall make a point of telling her that, inspector. See you in court, as they say – in the dock, I trust.' I turned and left before he could respond.

As we stepped into the sunlit shopping precinct outside the station, Alasdair said, 'Was that a threat, governor?'

'It was,' I said, 'but I shouldn't worry about it. Saffary isn't going to trouble anybody but his Chief Constable much longer. Come on, I need some of Ruby's tea and wads.'

From the Rendezvous I phoned Jayne with the good news, then slumped behind a table and attacked a plate of the usual and a large mug of tea. Alasdair sat opposite, sipping a cup of Earl Grey with lemon and rolling his evil-smelling cigarettes.

After a while he said, 'You were pretty good in there, boss.'

'Thanks,' I said. 'You weren't so bad yourself. How do you remember all those case references?'

'Nothing much else in the head.' He grinned. 'It was lucky, though – you spotting those tape marks on the diary. Without that they'd have had you on toast.'

I shook my head. 'Not luck,' I said. 'I was warned,' and I told him the whole story of Queenie's warning.

'What happens next?' he asked.

'I wish I knew. We've won the battle, Alasdair. They probably won't try me again, but Saffary was making clear that they'll try it with Sheila if they get the chance.'

I drank my tea, while Alasdair observed, 'You don't look like a bloke who's just screwed the most bent inspector in the force.'

'It's a deeply depressing thing to have hired killers trying to cripple you or burn you alive and bent coppers trying to jail you and ruin you professionally. Especially when you don't know why.'

I was depressed. I should have been exhilarated at the complete rout of Howard's and Saffary's vicious little plot, but I had been through too many days of strain, lately without the inspiration of Sheila beside me, and the present victory seemed very hollow.

'They won't try you again, will they governor?' my companion asked.

'Not if I keep to the middle of the pavement, public places and bright lights. My material with the Chief Constable will stymie any further police action or anything that an astute journalist might connect with today's events, but that doesn't mean the funnies aren't already arranging a convincing accident for me.'

'Doesn't seem to worry you,' Alasdair remarked.

'If they're going to try it, Al, there's little I can do to stop it, so there's no point in worrying about it. I'm more worried about Sheila. If I have convinced them into leaving me alone, they may turn their attentions on her, and I don't even know where she is at present.'

As soon as I said it I realised the truth of it. I might have saved myself at the price of exposing Sheila, and maybe that was what Saffary had meant. Now I was even more depressed.

We finished up and made for the office, entering by the front door from the square. A home-made 'Welcome Back' banner was pinned across the hall and while we stood and stared at it my teenage receptionist woke from her afternoon daydream and poked buttons on the intercom to warn the office of our return. Seconds later the narrow hall was full of the secretaries, Alan Reilly, Claude and the junior all beating Alasdair and me about the shoulders, applauding and cheering. In spite of my grey mood I was touched.

The mob flowed into the general office, which had been hastily draped with paper chains and balloons in a crude ball and chain pattern. Jayne's assistant, Mary Kendall, a solid, stocky redhead who could be just as formidable as Jayne but in a more ponderous and sinister style, produced a large cake, the iced top of which bore broad arrows and the inscription 'Property of Her Majesty's Prison'. Alan Reilly, who cultivates the bland appearance of a young, bemused curate, was thrusting glasses of white wine on everyone. When all had been supplied there were cries of 'Speech! Speech!'

I took up a position in front of the photocopier and raised my glass. 'I would like', I said, 'to thank my legal adviser, Mr Alasdair Thayne, the second-best criminal lawyer in the Midlands, for his moral back-up during my recent ordeal, and Mr Gordon Rains, aka Claude the Phantom, for his sterling efforts on my behalf. As to the rest of you, I am deeply grateful for your support, which I shall wear always . . .'

'I like the old jokes, too,' muttered Claude.

'. . . and merely wish to say that, if this was paid for out of the petty cash, it'll come out of your wages on Friday.'

More laughter and applause, above which Jayne announced, 'Actually we looked in the petty cash, but you took it all when you went to Wales, so we dipped into the lottery fund.'

The cake was cut and passed around. 'Mary,' I asked, 'how come you baked a cake?'

'Typed some of the stuff for the Chief Constable, didn't I?'

she said. 'And Jayne told me what she thought was going on, so I thought there might be a bit of a party when it was all over.'

'And what would have happened to this excellent cake if I'd been locked up?' I queried, through a mouthful.

'There's a hollow in the bottom for a file. We'd have brought it to the nick!'

The tail end of the afternoon passed in a blur of white wine and more old jokes, until Alan began to sing 'Midnight in Invertotty' and people began putting on coats. Soon there was just Alasdair and me, finishing off the last bottle of wine. I had already helped a number of other people finish off a number of other bottles during the afternoon, but I was not as drunk as I needed to be.

The fax machine beeped and began to creak into life, excreting a copy of a document headed by the impressive shield and supporters of the Central Midlands Police (Motto, *Fiat Justitia* – ho, bloody ho!). It was from an illegible signature on behalf of the Chief Constable, informing me that my letter and documents had been received and that, in view of the material they contained and my serious allegations, the Chief Constable had ordered 'urgent enquiries'. I would be informed of the result.

I passed it to Alasdair. 'Not bad,' he said when he'd read it. 'What do you imagine the result will be?'

'The result at the moment is that they're all sitting around in the bar at headquarters calling me filthy names and wondering how they can wriggle out of this one. The result that they'll tell me about in several weeks' time will be that they can't identify the fingerprints, their scientists don't agree with mine, they can't find who did it and that Howard has been sent on a twelve-month course with the FBI and Saffary has been moved to the post of Public Relations Officer.'

I drained my wine and Alasdair stood up. 'You sound as if it's time you went home,' he said.

'Oh, it is,' I agreed, 'it is. Come and help me move out of that damned hotel.'

'You're going back home?' he asked, surprised. 'Do you think that's a good idea?'

'Yes,' I said. 'I've been driven into Wales, chased all over the Principality, scared ragged, forced to live in the Victoria, and this morning I've had to look Howard and Saffary in their mean little eyes for ages. I've had enough, Al. Besides, I wouldn't put it past the sods to break in again tonight and plant some fresh bugs, Shergar's corpse, the missing Irish Crown Jewels and the proof that I was Jack the Ripper.'

He grinned. 'You're not old enough.'

'I feel it, Al. I feel it,' and I did.

An hour later he delivered me to my front gate. He was still anxious about my return, offering to stay with me. Normally I'd have welcomed his presence, but I needed to be alone with my worries and my guilt. We had a coffee in the kitchen, where Alasdair carefully dropped all the blinds before switching on the lights. Then he left.

I was desperate for Claude to call with Sheila's callback number, but he hadn't done so by half-past seven. Just before eight he rang to say there had been no message from her this evening. I remembered why we had gone to Wales in the first place, because they wanted to snatch her, and Saffary's veiled threat this morning. Suddenly I was afraid that they'd got her and there was nothing I could do about it.

I had thought that I was going to drop into my favourite armchair with a bottle of whisky and fret about Sheila till alcohol overwhelmed me, but it didn't work. If you've ever drunk alcohol to quell the pain of a toothache you'll know what I mean. You can absorb huge quantities of liquor without either getting drunk or dulling the pain.

By midnight I wasn't drunk and the pain wouldn't go away. In desperation I switched on the television, hoping that the late movie would bore me into a stupor. I'd missed the beginning, but it was about a bloke and his girl being chased all over a mountain and shot at. When the baddies captured the girl I switched it off.

There was nothing left to do but stare at the wall and imagine the worst. That was very successful, each worst I imagined being much worse than the one before.

Then there was a noise outside. Whatever alcohol was in my

151

bloodstream drained in a flash. Someone's foot had pressed very stealthily on the path at the side of the house, but not stealthily enough. The gravel had slid sufficiently to make a sound.

I doused the lamp on the table by my chair and soft-footed through into the kitchen. The drawn blinds made it almost pitch dark in there. Only the window in the back door gave a little light, but the tall bushes beyond it shaded it.

I crouched in the deep shadow behind the big kitchen table, watching the dim, striped oblongs of the right-hand blinds for a sign of somebody approaching outside. If someone had gone round the side path they must pass that window soon.

My imagination leapt back to life. I had been joking when I told Alasdair that they might break in again. I didn't really believe the police would have another try. But what about the smoothy, the expensively dressed character with the posh accent who chopped down old men and firebombed sleepers? Was he out there with a knife or a gun or his deadly, well-manicured hands? Had he dealt with Sheila and was he now about to tidy up the last loose end?

I could see the headline in tomorrow's *Express and Star*, telling how a Belston solicitor had been left dead when he disturbed a burglar at his home. I darted across the kitchen and coiled myself under the worktop alongside the back door. Maybe I could trip him as he came in and get some kind of advantage.

With one hand I reached up and groped on the worktop for a weapon. My fingers found a small chopping knife. Ideal for close stabbing, short and very sharp with a good point. I tried to remember every thriller I had ever read. Where was the best place to stab him? If he went down face upwards, should I stick it in his belly? In his heart? In his throat? If he fell the other way, what then? Wasn't there a point under the skull where you could stab directly into the brain? What if he didn't fall?

A faint movement caught my eye, reflected in the glass of the cupboards opposite. Someone was creeping past the window. I reached out again and softly turned the key back in the lock. I didn't want to make him force the door. I didn't know how

long that might take. Let him walk in, unsuspecting. That would give me the best chance.

The pale oblong on the tiled floor where the dim light from the door fell seemed darker. He was standing at the door. I breathed deeply.

There was a rap at the door. A 'shave-and-haircut-five-bob' knock. Loud and cheerful. Do hitmen knock before they enter? Is it part of the training? The knock came again, louder. Now I understood. He was finding out if I was awake, if there was going to be a struggle or whether he could kill me in my sleep.

I heard the doorknob rattle slightly and a pale line appeared on the floor as the door edged open. Then it swung wide, thudding against the cabinet on the other side. He was standing outside and I wasn't going to get a chance to trip him. He was too wary. In a moment he'd leap in, gun or deadly hands at the ready, and if I didn't hit the right spot with my knife immediately I was done for. I took another deep, silent breath and tensed myself for action.

Then there was a voice, a soft, low voice, calling, 'Chris? Chris Tyroll? Are you home?'

I uncoiled from my hiding-place as Sheila stepped through the door and switched on the light. In a second she was in my arms and I was clutching her and kissing her and weeping tears of relief down her neck. That went on for some time before I was able to let go of her and ask, 'What the hell are you doing here?'

'It's the boomerang in me,' she said. 'We always come back however far you chuck us.'

24

'You're drunk!' she accused, sniffing my breath.

'Oh no, I'm not,' I said. 'I might have been ten minutes ago, but the fright you gave me scared me stone cold sober! What the blazes made you sneak round to the back?'

'Paddy said he always came round the side and tapped the kitchen door.'

'True,' I said, 'but that's not usually at midnight when I'm drenched in whisky and paranoia.'

'I did scare you, didn't I?' she said, looking at my face, which was probably still about as white as the refrigerator.

She looked around and spotted the chopping knife which I had dropped when I realised who my visitor was.

'My oath!' she exclaimed. 'What were you going to do, Chris?'

'I thought the footsteps round the side were a house-call from the man in the sports jacket, so I decided to sell my life dearly.'

'Oh Chris, I'm sorry,' she said, and grabbed me again.

We were interrupted by a discreet cough at the open door. Paddy leaned against the doorpost, tweed hat in hand, knuckling his bald spot with his thumb.

'Hello there, Mr Tyroll,' he said. 'If you're all right now, miss, I'll be getting along.'

'No, you will not!' I said. 'Come in and tell me what you and Sheila are doing here at this time of night. I've been worried sick!'

Sheila, who will never get ulcers because her stomach remains unaffected by high drama, deathly danger or deep emotion, was already investigating my fridge and cupboards. 'Eggs, bacon and coffee, gents?' she offered.

In minutes we were all around the kitchen table eating and I found it hard to believe how recently I had been hiding behind it, expecting to die.

Paddy told me how he'd got worried for Sheila's sake.

'There was people dropping in at the camp,' he said, 'saying they was journalists and students and that, just wanting to talk to us or take photographs, they said.' He shook his head. 'They was no more students or journalists than I'm the President of America,' he said. 'I knew what they was after. So we started moving every day, a few miles, but some of them would still walk into the camp the next day and say, "Oh, here you are!" like they was surprised.'

He munched for a few moments in silence. 'So I had a talk witth old Queenie this afternoon,' he went on, as if there had been no pause. 'She agreed with me that the strangers was trouble for your young lady. She said you was out of your troubles and it was time the lady came back to you, you'd be better together now. So when it was full dark I brought her.'

He took a long swig at his mug of coffee and heaved himself out of his chair. 'That's it, Mr Tyroll,' he said, 'I brought her safe here and now I must be off.'

'Stay here, Paddy,' I said. 'Where have you got to get to?'

'We're up in Cheshire,' he said, 'but I can't stay. The boys'll be worrying if I'm not home by the morning. Thank you for the food and drink and goodnight to you both.'

His hat was jammed back on. I grabbed his hand and shook it warmly. 'I'll never be able to thank you enough, Paddy,' I said, 'and Martin and Miley and Queenie and all of them.'

'Ah, 'twas nothing at all,' he said. 'I'll see you when I'm about.'

'See that you do,' I said, 'and travel safely.'

In a second he was out of the back door and gone.

'Why were you drinking tonight?' Sheila asked.

'Because I have had a very hard day,' I said. 'By the time I got home I was tired, guilty, lonely and scared. And you didn't phone.'

She dropped her gaze. 'I didn't dare,' she said. 'You'd have told me not to come.'

I had to admit she was right. She reached across the corner of the table and clasped my hand. 'It wasn't just Paddy and Queenie, Chris. I wanted to be here. I got you into this and I wanted to be with you, whatever's happening.'

I was silent. I wanted her beside me, but I was remembering Saxon's warning and Saffary's veiled threat.

'What's more,' she said suddenly, 'Queenie Connors said I should be here. You said you never ignored her.'

I grinned and squeezed her hand. 'No more I would,' I said, 'but we're going to have to be damned careful.'

I told her what had happened since I arrived back in Belston, all the way down to Saffary's remarks.

All she said when I'd finished was, 'So old Queenie knew! How's she do it, Chris?'

'I think she's telepathic. She picks it out of your own mind, she knows what's worrying you and she finds the bit of your subconscious that knows what to do about it.'

Sheila nodded slowly. 'Yes,' she said, 'could be, but that doesn't explain how she knew about the planted fingerprints.'

'True, but I'm too tired to argue metaphysics with you.'

She stood up. 'Do they have hot showers and big double beds in Pommy houses?' she asked.

'Too right,' I said.

'Let's go,' she said, so we did.

Over breakfast we had decisions to make, like where Sheila could hole up. In the end we agreed that lying low at my place was as safe as anywhere we could think of. When I left for the office I had a list of groceries, clothing and feminine necessaries that Sheila had drawn up.

'Don't go shopping for them yourself,' she said, 'or every shop assistant in town'll think you're a pervert. Get Jayne to get them.'

I only had to give Jayne the list for her to look up and ask, 'Your raddled old academic's back in town, then?'

'Yes,' I said, 'but that's capital T Top, capital S Secret, OK?'

'Never heard it,' she said and slipped the list into her handbag.

Back at my desk I remembered an unfinished task – finding out if Norman Berry was still about. He would be too old to be still working at Kerrenwood's, but it occurred to me that a son might work there. I got the number from Enquiries and rang the plant, asking for Personnel.

When they answered I identified myself and told them I was looking for a witness in a pub fight. Another witness thought that the man was called Berry and worked at Kerrenwood's. Could they help me?

I heard computer keys tapping, then, 'Sorry, Mr Tyroll. There's nobody of that name working for us.'

'Perhaps he used to work for you,' I suggested. 'Could you check on that?'

'If he's on the Pension Fund, I could find him, but I couldn't give you his address.'

'That's all right,' I said. 'If you can confirm that there is such a man, I'll write to him care of Kerrenwood's and ask him to contact me.'

More tapping, then, 'No, I'm sorry, Mr Tyroll. There's no Berry on the Pension Fund either. Of course, he might have worked for us briefly and had no pension rights.'

I thanked her and gave up, puzzled. So, despite what Mrs Cassidy had said, Berry had never worked for Kerrenwood's. Still, thinking carefully, I realised that she hadn't said that. She'd said that Berry 'put Francy into a job' there. That might have been just influence, in Berry's case maybe blackmail.

I was still puzzling it over ten minutes later when the phone rang. Jayne had someone on the line who wouldn't state his business, but needed to speak to me urgently. It happens – they're embarrassed about being arrested in public lavatories or something, so they won't talk to a secretary.

I took the call. It was a man's voice that I didn't recognise. 'Is that Mr Christopher Tyroll? The solicitor?' it asked.

'Yes,' I said. 'This is Tyrolls, Jubilee Buildings, and this is Christopher Tyroll speaking. How can I help you?'

The line went dead. After a few moments I put the phone down and waited for the caller to ring back. He didn't. I buzzed Jayne and asked if he had.

'No,' she said, 'but I meant to ask – was it someone you know?'

'No, why?'

'Because he called in on the unlisted line. I thought you must have given him the number.'

I sat and looked at the phone and puzzled for minutes before I realised. I had called Kerrenwood's on the ex-directory line and a stranger had called in on it. To check whose it was. I'd made a mistake in giving my name to Kerrenwood's – but what kind of mistake?

157

The episode made me uneasy and disturbed my morning's work, but just before lunchtime John Parry arrived with a bag of sandwiches from the Rendezvous, a bottle of wine and a newspaper.

When Jayne showed him in he was grinning broadly. 'Thought I'd deliver the good news in person,' he said and dropped the newspaper on my desk.

It was the early edition of the *Express and Star* and the second lead on the front page was accompanied by a photograph of Superintendent Howard. BELSTON POLICE CHIEF RETIRES, said the headline, and the paragraphs below explained that Howard was taking early retirement because 'recent changes in the criminal law have made the work of the police more difficult and given further advantages to criminals. I no longer feel that I can remain a police officer.'

I read the remark aloud and looked up at Parry. He was still grinning. 'Saw himself as Commissioner of the Met, he did,' he said.

'Well, since about this time yesterday,' I said, 'he has known that he wasn't even going to make Chief Superintendent. Anyway, why are you so happy? They're not going to give you his job.'

'No, not yet,' he said, 'but it's an ill wind. You see before you Acting Detective Inspector Parry. That's what the wine's for.'

'And how did that come about? Have they sacked Saffary?'

'No such luck, boyo, but rumour says he has been sent to reflect upon his misdeeds in the Traffic Cones Store.'

Jayne, who had spotted John's bottle, appeared with glasses and joined us in a toast to his promotion. When she had gone he put down his glass.

'There's another bit of what might be good news,' he said. 'Since Saffary's reassignment, I'm back on the Brown and Cassidy case.'

'Is that good news?' I said, churlishly.

He looked at me evenly. 'I had a pep-talk from the Divisional Chief Super this morning. Says he wants the case wrapped up quickly.'

'And what, exactly, does he mean by that?'

158

He unwrapped the sandwiches and selected a thick ham one before replying. 'I think he means that I'm to find some little runt in a leather jacket who's got a bit of form for assault and persuade him to confess.'

That was about what I thought, too. Moodily I took a sandwich. 'And is that what you propose to do?' I asked.

He refused to be riled. 'Not exactly, no,' he said from behind his sandwich. 'I was thinking more of finding an ex-army type with a blue car and a button off his sports coat.'

'And what'll you do when you find him?'

'I'll check his DNA against the specimen from the old man's walking-stick, and when they match I'll charge him with murder. If I can get the staff at the home to identify him, I'll charge him for Francy Cassidy as well.'

'And you know what'll happen then?' I said. 'He'll make one phone call and in minutes there'll be a call from Whitehall to the Chief Constable with "national security" repeated several times in an expensive accent. Five minutes after that you'll be told to let him go.'

He opened his mouth but I overrode him. 'And if you're daft enough to refuse – and you might be – the Crown Prosecution Service will take over the case and discontinue the prosecution. You'll never get made up to full Inspector and not a word'll appear in the press because there'll be a D Notice slapped on it by the Home Office.'

'You may be right,' he said, 'but I don't want you and Sheila saying I didn't try. I can't hang him myself, you know.'

'No, of course not,' I said. 'I'm sorry, John. After Saffary and Howard I'm a bit cynical perhaps. Pour us another.'

He refilled our glasses and we ate silently for a minute or two. Then I asked, 'Saffary said he was treating Sheila as a suspect. I take it you don't want to see her again?'

'That', he said, 'was his idea of a veiled threat. Subtle sort of bloke was Saffary. No, Chris, I don't regard her as a suspect. Where is she, by the way?'

'Is that an official question?'

'No, no,' he said, 'just wondered.'

'She's safe,' I said, 'I think.'

'I'm glad,' he said. 'Have a buttered bun,' and pushed the sandwich bag across.

At the day's end I went home loaded with Jayne's purchases and told Sheila the good news. She was sitting in my study, with the desk covered in the contents of her grandfather's tin box, the two versions of the Victory photograph and her notes. A pad beside her was covered with scribbled questions and partly completed tables of facts.

'Are you getting anywhere?' I asked.

'No,' she said and flung down her pencil. 'I can't find any kind of pattern in it, apart from the facts that out of the guys in the photograph too many seem to have died or vanished and that the death of one of them was connected with Grandpa's murder and that there was something queer about the landlord's ration book which Grandpa knew about and they're all waving ration books in the picture. What's that all mean, Chris?'

'I don't know,' I said. 'But Queenie said, "Look in the picture."'

'I've looked in this damned picture till I'm blue in the face,' she complained. 'I know everything in it.'

'Do you think', I said, 'that there could be things in it we're not seeing?'

'How do you mean?' she said.

'I mean both of those prints are old and yellowed. Do you think if we had it computer-enhanced it might show us something we're missing?'

'Grandpa's eyes can't have been all that good,' she said. 'He was eighty-five. If he could see what's in it, we ought to be able to.'

'Maybe he didn't have to look for information in it. Perhaps he already knew what it meant from Jim Brown.'

She frowned down at the prints. 'Maybe,' she conceded. 'Is Brown still around?'

I shook my head. 'I had Alan Reilly check. Brown died about a couple of months ago, so that probably was where your grandfather got the photo and he must have known what it meant.'

She stood up wearily. 'I am going to shower and change and stop looking like a tinker's mot and while I'm doing that, you're going to get the grub on. As to the picture – if you think that computer-whatchermecalling it will do any earthly good, have a go. I'm beginning to think we've got about Buckley's chance of finding anything in it.'

25

I used to know about computers. That was back in the days when words came up on your screen asking you what you wanted it to do and telling you which key to press for it. Then you pressed the right key and it did what you wanted. Then it all changed so that now you get screen after screen that you don't want and it takes you six unnecessary moves to get where you're going and each screen is dotted about with silly pictures that don't remind you of anything and this is progress and is making Bill Gates a hell of a lot of money. So I just stick to the simple stuff on the office system and a word-processor at home.

Alasdair, on the other hand, loves computers. He wasn't happy with the boring old terminal in his room at the office, so he imported at his own expense a couple of thousand quid's worth of machine with drive slots and lights all over it and stereo speakers and a modem and things. It's linked into our system, but at lunchtimes he's playing three-dimensional chess on the Internet with a schoolboy in New Zealand and in the evenings he engages in romantic chat with a lady in Seattle who's probably a frustrated transvestite truck-driver in real life.

Next morning I showed him the pictures and asked him about computer enhancement.

'What are you looking for, boss?' he asked.

'I don't know,' I said. 'Anything at all that's in that picture. I want a bloke who can extract every last drop of information from it. I want to be able to see the pattern on the wallpaper and the fag ash on the floor.'

'Pete could do it,' he said.

'Who's Pete?'

'He's a tech assistant at Wolverhampton Uni.'

I picked up the phone. 'Ring him,' I said. 'Tell him it's urgent. Tell him I'll pay whatever he asks.'

Eventually he tracked Pete down on the phone and talked computer slang at him for several minutes.

'He says he'll start this afternoon if you want to bring the pictures over – and the money. Fifty up front and maybe more later.'

Afternoon found me waiting for Pete by the Scott Library at the university. At last he came out of the library's doors and held out his hand.

'I'm Pete,' he said. 'You must be Alasdair's boss.'

He was a throwback, all long unkempt hair and beard, tatty flared jeans and evil-coloured shirt.

He led me away through long corridors and up stairs, turning at last into what looked like some kind of science laboratory. Beyond the lab he pushed open a door marked 'Staff Only' and showed me into a gloomy, cluttered space, lit by the flickering gaudy light of several computer monitors. I should have guessed from the clothing that his workspace would reek of marijuana.

He dropped into an office chair and pointed me to another. 'Now,' he said, 'what's this picture that's such a problem?'

I passed him both prints and he swivelled his chair, switched on a desk lamp and examined them closely.

After a bit he said, 'Right. Two prints of the same picture. Both a bit faded. Taken about fifty years ago from the clothes. What do you want to know?'

'All I know about that picture', I said, 'is the identities of the people in it and the pub in which it was taken. That came from someone who knew them all, but she doesn't know exactly why or when it was taken. I need to know everything at all that you can extract from either print that doesn't meet the naked eye.'

'Right,' he said again. 'Both about the same quality. I'll scan them both on to disc and we'll see which one works best.'

While the pictures ran on a flatbed scanner he dug around in the gloom and produced leads with which he began to connect equipment. Two more screens, larger than the others, lit up at the far end of the room. One had a keyboard in front of it.

'Right,' he said. 'It's on disc. Now I'll put it up on the big screens and you can see what we've got.'

I walked down to the big screens and watched as a dark stripe washed rapidly across both, leaving behind it an enlarged version of the photograph.

'Large screen monochrome,' he said from behind me. 'Sit at that one and I'll work at this one. That way you can see what I'm doing without getting in the way.'

We settled in chairs and I noticed that he had a large, untidy cigarette in his mouth. He drew on it hard for a few seconds, then said, 'You're not interested in the blokes' faces?'

'You can print anything that's on screen, can't you?' I asked.

'Right,' he agreed. 'The whole picture. Any part of it. Enlarged or reduced. Tell me if you want something printing. Do you want the faces?'

'I know who they are, but a set of reference prints might be handy.'

The screen went into close-up on each face in turn as he manipulated a mouse across his desk. Each face appeared in crisp enlargement, then a couple of clicks on the mouse and the printer whirred into life.

'What next?' he said, as the last sheet dropped from the printer.

'I don't know,' I said. 'Perhaps if you work over the whole picture in enlargement we'll get some ideas.'

'Is this a party?' he asked. 'It's obviously a pub, and in the Midlands.'

'It's some kind of party,' I said. 'How are you sure it's in the Midlands?'

'Look,' he said and zoomed in on a pale patch on the left wall. 'If I'm right,' he said, 'that's an old Ansells advert.'

'Good,' I said. 'We think it's a VE Day party.'

'At the end of the war?' he said. 'Doesn't look like it.'

'Why not?' I asked, surprised.

'No decorations,' he said. 'No bunting, no flags.'

163

'There'd been a war on,' I said.

'Right,' he said, 'and I've seen pictures of street parties. Masses of bunting, flags, streamers. They knew it was ending, you know.'

He clicked about with the mouse again. 'Look at that,' he directed.

A vague dark-outlined rectangle on the rear wall leapt into view as a framed portrait of King George VI in peaked cap and army uniform. 'No decorations,' he said again. 'You'd have thought they'd at least put a bit of something round His Majesty.'

He scanned on across the rear wall, pausing at the clock. 'Either it's stopped,' he said, 'or this was illegal boozing,' as the clock face swelled on the screen. The hands quite clearly showed five minutes to four.

'They were all pals of the landlord,' I said. 'What's that?'

I had seen a pale, oblong object appear out of a shadowed corner at the back, something standing on an unoccupied table.

'A box, I think,' he said. More clicks and it enlarged. It appeared to be a cardboard carton, with its top flaps opened, standing corner-on to the camera.

'Can you get the writing on the side?' I asked.

He closed in on the side. There was a roundish, black blob with two broken lines underneath, seemingly the labelling on the long side of the carton. He brightened the image and darkened it, shrank it and enlarged it, but the angle of the box to the camera was too great. The label wouldn't resolve. At last he froze on a medium shot.

'Best you'll get,' he said, apologetically. 'Black blob at the top with something light on it. Three words underneath, probably. Long one, short one, medium one. Two larger, medium words below that. Any good?'

'Print it,' I said, and the printer whirred again. I had no idea what it meant, if anything.

'Go for the ration books,' I suggested.

A book cover appeared, filling half the screen. The Ministry of Food badge and the black print on what would have been a pale buff background were pretty clear. Every word was legible, but there was nothing in the spaces for the holder's name and address.

'Why doesn't the handwriting show up?' I asked.

'What handwriting?'

'There should be a handwritten name and address, on the dotted lines,' I said.

He played with brightness, contrast, size, but nothing appeared.

'There's nothing there,' he said at last.

'There's got to be,' I said. 'They were filled in when they were issued.' A thought struck me. 'Could it be that the ink's too pale? I see a lot of old forms and they used to use really watery ink in some government offices.'

'Shouldn't be that bad,' he said. He continued to tweak the image of the cover, but nothing appeared.

He moved on to the other ration books. They were all the same. None of them showed a trace of handwriting.

'I suppose the camera flash might have blanked out a pale blue ink,' he said, not very convinced by his own arguments.

'Look,' I said, 'I've got to be back in Belston, but you're doing fine. Do me a set of prints of the best images you can get of the book covers and anything else at all that you think may help me find out what was happening in that picture.'

A thought occurred to me. 'Some of these characters are dead,' I said, 'but some aren't or may not be. Can you alter their appearances? Can you give me an idea of what they might look like now – fifty years on? Fatter or thinner, with or without beards, bald or whatever? Is it possible?'

'Possible,' he confirmed, 'but it'll cost you.'

I gave him a hundred. 'That's a retainer,' I said. 'I'll pay whatever it costs.'

He grew more enthusiastic. 'When do you want this stuff?'

'If you can carry on with it and send anything you print over to my office by courier tomorrow, I'll pay fifty per cent over the rate.' I gave him my card and identified the Cassidy brothers and Alan Thorpe as dead and not worth attention.

Picking up the pile of prints from the printer tray I stuffed them into my briefcase and shook his hand. 'Tomorrow morning,' he confirmed, smiling and reaching for his cigarette papers.

Twenty minutes later I had found my way out to the street.

I took Alasdair home with me when the office closed. We dined well and over the second bottle of Alasdair's wine Sheila began chewing our problem all over again. Alasdair listened carefully to her theories and comments.

I got Pete's prints out of my briefcase and explained his comments.

'Not a Victory party?' queried Sheila. 'What else is it, then?'

'Could be any time,' Alasdair said. 'It's a good point about the decorations.'

'Come on, you two!' said Sheila. 'These blokes were shysters, small-time racketeers profiting out of the war. They weren't exactly patriotic. What'd they care about King and Country?'

'True,' I said, 'but Jim Brown had a living to make and his other customers might have expected a bit of patriotic display.'

We chased that around for a bit and got nowhere. Then I showed them the blurry print of the box.

'So what?' said Sheila. 'It's a cardboard box. Big deal. The booze was in it. One of the black marketeers brought the whisky in for the party.'

'Maybe,' I said, and took out the pictures of the ration book covers. I explained how hard Pete had tried to bring out any writing on any of them. Sheila looked puzzled. Alasdair rolled a cigarette and looked at each cover in turn. Then he looked up at me.

'You've got a theory about this, haven't you, governor?'

'Yes,' I said. 'I think they're forgeries.'

'Could you forge a ration book?' he asked. 'Weren't there any security traps? You know, like the jolly old metal bit in banknotes?'

'I don't know,' I said.

Sheila got up from the table and came back with her grandfather's ration book and the James Brown one. She put them on the table.

'Can anyone tell the difference?' she asked.

I picked up Walter Brown's book and leafed through it. At least that one was genuine.

'The cover's fairly ordinary thin card,' I said, 'but the coupons are printed on soft, rough paper.' I held it up to the light. 'I think it's got hairs in it, like American banknotes. It's a very distinctive paper.'

Alasdair took it from me and compared it, page by page, with the James Brown book.

'They seem identical to me,' he said. 'The paper even feels the same. If one's a forgery, it's a damned good one!'

'And we don't even know if it is a forgery,' I pointed out. 'That might be Jim Brown's real ration book.'

'My oath!' exclaimed Sheila. 'My head's spinning. Who's for coffee?'

Nobody said anything while we drank our coffee, then Alasdair took out his tin and rolled a cigarette. Once it was smoking nicely, he removed some fragments of tobacco from his tongue and looked at both Sheila and me in turn.

'Look,' he began, more nervously than I was used to with him. 'I know that I'm new to this and you've been turning it round for days, but sometimes a fresh eye sees things that have got sort of, well forgotten.'

'Like what?' I said.

'Well, when this all began, Sheila came to the office because she couldn't find her grandfather and his letter said that you knew what it was all about, didn't she?'

'Right,' I said, 'but I didn't. Walter Brown never mentioned a word of this to me, I promise you.'

'I know,' he said, 'but he wrote that because he thought old age might have caught up on him before Sheila got here.'

'Yes,' I said, not seeing where this was going.

'So he thought you'd be dealing with his will in that case. What's in the will?'

'Sheila's seen the will,' I said.

'Hold on a minute!' she said slowly. 'You gave me a photo-copy of the will out of your file. You said the real will, the signed original was in your whatchermecally.'

'The deeds cabinet,' I said. 'Yes, and we couldn't get at it because our nasties firebombed the filing room and the heat jammed the lock, but it doesn't matter – you've seen exactly what it says.'

'That's not what I meant, governor,' said Alasdair. 'Didn't you tell me that Mr Brown called one day just to look at his will and you couldn't think why because you thought he'd have known exactly where his own copy was?'

'Yes, and he did. It was in his tin box.'

Sheila's eyes lit up. 'You're right!' she said to Alasdair. 'Don't you see, Chris? He came in because he wanted to put something in with his will! Something you and I would find if he died. I told you that you should have read it out properly to me and Mrs Croft round a long table!'

She jumped up, clasped Alasdair's face and kissed him. 'Alasdair Thayne,' she said, 'you're a beaut!'

'Do you know,' I admitted, 'I think the boy's right! But I'm not going to kiss you, Al, because there's still a problem. The deeds cabinet is still jammed shut.'

Alasdair was smiling anyhow, but it broadened. 'Not so,' he said. 'While you two were enjoying yourselves playing tag in Wales, I was harassing the locksmith. The lock has been in working order for days!'

'What are we waiting for?' said Sheila, and we all stood up.

Alasdair dropped us in front of the office minutes later. 'I shan't come in,' he said. 'I think this is really for you two. See you in the morning. You can tell me all about it.'

I walked up the side alley by the office. Sheila lingered to give Alasdair another congratulatory kiss, at least, I hoped it was congratulatory.

I stepped into the darkened rear yard and took a pace forward before it registered. There are security lights on the back of my building. I put them there to discourage local youths from using the yard as a fornicatorium after the pubs shut. They respond to movement and they should have switched on when I rounded the corner. They hadn't.

I stopped dead and peered into the gloom. Across the far

side of the yard a familiar dark car was parked. It was too dark to see its colour, but I knew that it was dark blue.

26

I shot back down the alley in time to stop Sheila entering the yard. I was too late to stop Alasdair leaving. I could hear his car turning out of the square.

I drew Sheila in against the wall and hissed at her not to speak. It didn't entirely work. 'What's up?' she whispered.

'They're in the office,' I said, 'our friends. The blue car's parked in the yard and someone's disabled the security lights.'

'What are you going to do?'

'I'm going to find out whereabouts they are, first of all,' I whispered.

'Don't take any stupid risks, Chris,' she commanded.

'Stay here,' I said. 'I'll be back.'

I stepped stealthily back into the yard and edged silently along the near side, keeping deep in the shadow of the wall. As my eyes became accustomed to the darkness I could see that the door at the top of the fire escape was standing open. There should have been a pale oblong where the cream door stood closed, but there was a black one where it was open. The pale glow of a torch or something similar illuminated the filing room window faintly. It looked like they'd had the same thought as us.

I dropped back into the alley and took my keys from my pocket.

'Here', I said to Sheila, 'is a front door key.' I detached a bronze key from the ring and put it in her hand. 'Open the front door quietly and slip in. Can you find the reception door on the right in the dark?'

'Yes,' she said.

'Good! Then slip into reception. There's a phone on the

right-hand end of the receptionist's desk. The emergency number's . . .'

'. . . 999,' she said. 'I know.'

'It's a push button phone with a big block of nine buttons and a separate one at the bottom. That's the zero, so the nine's the bottom right corner of the big block. Just tell the police there are armed burglars at 24a Jubilee Buildings. Then get out of the front door again – and lock it!'

'What if they're inside the front door with machine guns?'

'They're not,' I said. 'They're two floors up in the filing room.' I didn't tell her I intended to distract them.

She wasn't just the most beautifully freckled face in the world. She gave me a quick kiss and slid off down the alley. All guts, my Doctor of Social History.

I moved back into the yard and approached the fire escape. I willed the hundred-year-old tower of rust not to creak or clang as I began to creep stealthily up it.

Keeping well into the wall side seemed to work. Only a few quiet groans came from the old ironwork as I soft-footed upwards. Nobody popped a head out of the door to look.

At last I was at the top. One step below the top landing. By now Sheila should be on the phone. My next move was to step quickly into the open doorway at the top of the fire escape, pull the solid Victorian door shut and lock it. However good they were, by the time they got through that I'd be well out of range and with a little luck the police would be here.

I stepped quickly on to the top landing and into the open doorway, crouching and reaching inwards for the door handle as I did so. I had just touched it when a voice spoke.

'Welcome aboard, Mr Tyroll!' it said, in well-bred tones. 'Just stay exactly where you are or I'll blow you out of the doorway.'

I stayed, crouched with my hand extended to the doorknob. Something moved in the dark interior corridor. A shape appeared against the stairhead window at the other end of it. It moved towards me and, as it got nearer, I could see that it was a tall man with a gun in his hand.

Two paces from me he stopped. Now I could just distinguish the sports jacket.

'Take your hand off the doorknob,' he commanded, 'and raise them both over your head.' I did so. 'Now step very slowly into the passage.'

I advanced towards him, hands high.

'Back very slowly into the door behind you,' he said, indicating the filing room door with a movement of his gun.

'Stop,' he commanded, when I was standing in the doorway. A faint light was filtering from the filing room and I could hear someone clanking metal objects. His mate, no doubt, working on the deeds cabinet.

The light shone on the pistol's rim and I could see how big the mouth of the weapon was. I have never been so frightened in my life. In the very near future I was going to become a statistic. An unlucky, dead solicitor, who happened to call at his office out of hours and was killed because he disturbed burglars. Case unsolved. Or they'd leave a few faked clues and poor old Warren and his boys would go down for killing me in the course of a piece of political sabotage.

He stepped forward, pointing the gun straight at my face. I swallowed hard.

Something hurtled out of the dark corridor and slammed him sideways. With a startled cry he disappeared through the open fire escape door and I heard the gun thud down on to the floor. Before I could react there was a loud crack from outside and another strangled cry, followed by an echoing crash.

I dived into the doorway, scooping up the gun as I did so. Sheila was huddled to the left of the door, clinging to the old iron railing and panting. The metalwork swayed as I stepped out of the door.

'Don't,' said Sheila. 'It's not safe!'

It certainly wasn't. The far side rail and the whole section of outer rail to the last flight had been carried away. I peered gingerly down into the yard. Something lay huddled on the cobbles below. It wasn't moving.

I took Sheila's hand and began to draw her into the building when I heard a movement behind me.

When somebody holds a pistol in your face and you think you're going to die at any moment it frightens and humiliates

171

you and swamps you with useless adrenalin. If you live, there's a reaction. All that adrenalin and the relief make you very angry.

I leapt into the filing room door brandishing the gun. In the light of an electric lantern on the floor I could see a small man in a leather jacket. He was crouched by the deeds cabinet, bundling tools into a canvas holdall. I slammed the light switch down and thrust the gun at him as he blinked in the light.

'Get up!' I shouted. 'Put your hands up and stand against that wall!' I've never felt more like killing someone in my life. The man who'd frightened me was two floors down and out cold, but I needed something to compensate for my terror.

There was a fusillade of loud knocks at the front door. An amplified voice yelled, 'Armed police! Open up!' Two police cars shot into the yard, blue lights flashing and sirens yelping like hounds.

'Switch all the lights on,' I told Sheila, 'and open the front door – slowly and carefully so they don't shoot you. I'll look after this little bastard.'

Heavy feet sounded on the bottom of the fire escape. 'Don't!' I shouted. 'The top handrail's broken. It's not safe!' They stopped. There were voices down below, inside and out, and more feet coming up the stairs.

John Parry's voice sounded behind me. 'Citizen's arrest is it, Mr Tyroll? I think you can give me the gun now.'

I passed it over my shoulder to him and my hand began to shake as I released the weapon.

Parry slipped past me into the room. 'What's your name?' he snapped at the man in the leather jacket.

'Gibson,' he said, 'Frank Gibson,' at a second attempt when he had got his voice working. I felt a nasty satisfaction at knowing that other people were scared when someone pointed a big ugly pistol at them.

'Frank Gibson,' recited Parry, 'you are under arrest for breaking and entering with intent to commit an indictable offence and for possible other offences including murder or aiding and abetting murder. You do not have to say anything,

172

but your defence may be harmed if you do not mention anything which you later rely on in court. Anything you do say may be given in evidence.'

He slid the gun into his pocket and turned away. 'Take him, lads,' he said to two officers who stood in the corridor.

'Now,' he said brightly, 'since that's a crime scene, is there somewhere we can have a chat about all this?'

I led him and Sheila down to my own office, sat them down and went in search of the Birthdays Bottle in Jayne's desk. Parry eyed it when I returned with three glasses.

'Don't give me the "No thank you, sir – I'm on duty" bit,' I said.

'I was about to remark', he said, 'that I was just off shift when Sheila's call came in, so I am here voluntarily, which I think permits me to accept an offer of refreshment.'

I poured three large ones. Sheila was white, her freckles standing out like paint, but a treble whisky, swallowed without pause, restored her colour. Parry took his in three gulps and stood up.

'Have a rest,' he said. 'I've got to go and talk to my lads.'

When he'd gone, I lifted my glass to Sheila. 'You saved my life,' I said.

She grinned. 'I told you,' she said. 'No one's going to shoot you and stuff you except me, Chris Tyroll.' Then she came round the desk at me and suddenly all the fear and anger was disappearing as she wrapped herself about me.

Some time afterwards John Parry coughed at the door. 'Wonderful,' he remarked, 'the effects of alcohol on the inexperienced.'

He dropped into a chair. 'Tell me about it,' he said.

We explained about the rambling discussion at my home, Alasdair's input and the decision to visit the office.

'And you were so full of Al Thayne's wine', he said, 'that when you found you'd got a couple of Her Majesty's killers on the premises you decided to sort them out yourself?'

'No,' I said. 'I just meant to lock the fire escape door so as to delay them till you got here.'

He shook his head. 'A long time ago,' he said, 'I warned you to leave it alone. What's the use of me making Inspector if the public goes about arresting killers?'

He was serious again. 'The man with the gun,' he said. 'Do you know his name?'

'He never introduced himself,' I said.

'No. Well, he wouldn't. According to the majority of the identification he had on him, his name's Naylor.'

'What department?' I asked.

'That', said Acting Inspector Parry, 'is an Official Secret, Mr Tyroll, the answer to which I cannot give you. Suffice it to say that his superiors have been informed already and have already said that they can't imagine why he was in Belston.'

'What's he saying?' asked Sheila.

Parry gazed at her. 'He's not saying anything, love. He broke his neck when he hit the yard.'

I looked quickly at Sheila to see how she took the news. Her grey eyes widened slightly, but her voice was steady.

'Good,' she said, 'exactly what he did to Grandpa. Now your bosses can't let the murdering swine off.'

We settled down to making statements while one of John's DCs supplied us with coffee. It was daylight by the time we finished.

Parry slid the statement forms into his document case and stood up.

'That's it,' he said. 'You're not going to have any bother over this. When Naylor's DNA has been checked I shall put him on the file as the killer of Walter Brown. Gibson will confess to me his part in the Cassidy murder.'

'You're sure he will?' I asked.

'Oh, yes, I'm very sure. When he does I shall charge him with aiding and abetting the murders of Walter Brown and Francy Cassidy. No one's going to stop me doing that.'

'What'll he get?' asked Sheila.

'Life,' he said, 'twice over. We charge accessories as principals. Killing two old men should guarantee a judge's recommendation for a minimum of twenty years. Now go home to bed.'

174

We did, and lay sleepless. After a long time Sheila began to cry silently until at last she slept.

27

It seemed to be only seconds before the alarm woke me. I banged it off and willed myself to stay awake until I could phone Jayne at home. I managed to make it and warn her that there would probably be coppers crawling all over the filing room and the fire escape all day, that the press would be making her life a misery, and that I wasn't coming in to the office and I wasn't taking any phone calls before sleep overcame me again.

It was late morning when I woke again. Sheila was ahead of me, showered and in the kitchen brewing up.

After breakfast I stretched my legs luxuriously under the kitchen table. 'I have told Jayne', I said, 'that I am not appearing in the office today. We can have a day of rest.'

'No chance!' she exclaimed. 'Aren't you forgetting a couple of things?'

'What things?'

'In the midst of all the drama last night, we never did get to see if Grandpa left anything in the deeds cabinet, did we?'

'True.'

'And you're expecting a parcel from Pete the computer genius, aren't you?'

'True.'

'Well, get your shoes on, cobber. There's work to do.'

As we arrived at the office a motor-cycle courier was walking out to his machine.

Jayne had put the package from Pete on my desk. I opened it and began to sort through it. The first item a typed schedule of figures. A note at the bottom said, 'Figures, apparently scores, extracted from blackboard, left side of dartboard, left-hand wall.' I admired his thoroughness and turned over.

175

Next was an enlarged print with a typescript clipped to the back. The print showed part of the dartboard and the right-hand scoreboard adjacent to it. Something was scrawled there in large chalked capitals. I couldn't read it, but the attached note read, 'Writing on blackboard, right side of dartboard, left-hand wall, apparently darts fixture.' Pete had tried hard to decipher it and transcribed it as:

L.B. LEAGUE

T--- SUNDAY

-AG-E & P-M-

v

T-- B-LL

2.30

PL--S- -- --

T--E!!

I didn't see anything in that either, but underneath it was a thick wad of prints of faces. He had really gone to town on those. He had taken Watson and Thompson and Berry as they appeared in the photograph and tried every way of ageing them by fifty years. There were several versions of each face, thin old men with bald heads, thin old men with thick silver hair, wrinkly-faced old men, smoothy-chops old men, fat-faced old men, old men with moustaches and beards, old men in every variety of spectacles – the variety was bewildering.

I was passing the face prints across to Sheila, but she was scarcely glancing at them.

'While you're playing Photofit,' she said, after a bit, 'do you think I could look for Grandpa's will?'

I gave her my key-ring and pointed out the deeds cabinet key. 'They're all in alphabetical order, each in a sealed brown envelope. It should be near the top being a B. When you've got it, lock the cabinet again and bring it down.'

My desk was awash with Pete's adventures in physiognomy when Alasdair walked in, back from court.

'I hear you had quite an exciting night after I dropped you off,' he said. 'Sorry I didn't stay, but I didn't know there was going to be any fisticuffs.'

'There wasn't,' I said. 'There was a lot of creeping about in the dark by myself and Sheila, a certain amount of waving guns and making threats by Mr Naylor and then he met with an unfortunate accident.'

'Naylor must be the government chappy? The spy or whatever?'

'He was,' I confirmed. 'He was also the swine who killed Walter Brown, and Sheila had the considerable consolation of chucking him off the fire escape and breaking his bloody neck. Not that she meant to,' I added, 'she was saving my neck at the time.'

'Nice lady, Sheila,' he said. 'Does you good, governor. You really ought to keep her about.'

'If people are going to go on bombing me and shooting at me, I shall.'

'And are they?'

'Are they what?'

'Going to go on with the bombing and all that? Do you know any more about it?'

'No,' I admitted, 'but Sheila's upstairs looking for her grand-father's will. That might tell us something.'

I extracted another clip of documents from Pete's package. This time it was another set of ration book covers, full-page size. Across the top one he had scribbled, 'Not a trace on any of them – these books have not been written on.'

I showed it to Alasdair. He riffled through them for a moment, then said, 'Forgeries, then. You were right.'

'But are a few forged ration books that important after fifty years? And it can't have been more than a few. Either they nicked some of that special paper or – most unlikely – they managed to imitate it. Either way, it can't have been a big operation.'

Sheila came back and laid a sealed envelope on my desk. I

broke the seal and drew out Walter Brown's original will. As I unfolded it a paper dropped out, written in the old man's clerkly hand.

I picked it up and gave it to Sheila. 'There it is,' I said. 'You read it.'

She read it to herself with a look of growing puzzlement, then she read it aloud, slowly:

My dear Sheila,

If you have received this from my solicitor then it will only be because time has caught up on me too soon or because events have gone wrong. Since I began what I have been doing I have had some funny phone calls and once or twice I've thought I was being followed, but maybe I'm just old and imagining things.

I told you that I wanted to put something right if I was spared. It was something from the war, when I was at the Town Hall. I was blamed for the robbery at Renton Street, despite the fact that there were fire-watchers on that building every night, but they were knocked out when it was robbed and I was blamed. Perhaps it was my fault, but in the war we had to do a lot of things in a hurry and sometimes they went wrong.

What was even worse was that the government wouldn't let the police take any action, so that the public wouldn't know. That was quite wrong. Those that did it should have been brought to justice, but they never were.

Sergeant Reynolds had a suspicion that a man called Francis Cassidy drove the lorry, but his superiors wouldn't let him do anything about it. Now I know two things. I have a picture of the men who did it and I have found out where Cassidy is. Perhaps, after all the years, I can see that the world knows who was the rotten traitor that did it. He must have made a fortune. I suppose he is long gone, but that isn't the point. He should never have been allowed to profit by it. In other countries he would have been shot or hanged.

That's what it has been about, Sheila. The photograph is in my 'funny book' as you used to call it and young Tyroll

178

will be able to tell you all about Renton Street if he checks up.

I am sorry that we shall not meet again in this world, my dear, but you have always had,

All my love,

Your grandfather.

Her cheeks were wet before she finished and silently handed the letter back to me.

'He wrote that because he was becoming frightened,' I said. 'They knew that he was trying to rock somebody's boat.'

'But it had been years,' said Alasdair. 'They can't have kept watch all that time! How did they know he was going to dig it up again?'

'Francy Cassidy,' I said. 'He was in an old folks' home. He might have gone gaga at any time and started babbling about it. They must have taken precautions against that. All they had to do was bung a few quid to the underpaid kids who do all the work there. You know, a concerned member of the family wants an eye kept on him, who comes to visit him, asks about him, that sort of thing. Nothing mattered till Walter found Cassidy, then it was killing time.'

'But why didn't they stop then?' asked Alasdair.

'They were going to,' I said. 'Even if Sheila came over from Oz, they didn't think she'd catch on. But she got here too soon and she came to see me. So they watched us. They took a swipe at me in an anonymous sort of way by way of discouraging me, but they really went wild when we caught on to Cassidy and tried to see him. After that we were targets. When they lost us in Wales they got Howard and Saffary to do their dirty work on me if I showed up. That would have discredited me and probably put me inside. Then they could work on Sheila.'

Alasdair nodded, but Sheila grimaced. 'But what is it all about?' she said, exasperatedly. 'I don't know what that letter means and I can't see that a few forged ration books fifty years ago is worth all the killing!'

'Someone talked about Renton Street,' I remembered. 'Mrs Cassidy? No! Sergeant Reynolds! That's it!'

I snatched up the phone, then realised that I had neither a phone number nor an address for the old copper. I didn't even know his daughter-in-law's surname.

A moment's thought gave me an idea. I rang Belston CID office and got John Parry.

'John,' I said, 'I need a phone number for Sergeant Reynolds, you know? The oldest surviving Belston copper? If you can get me one, I might finally be able to work out what this is all about.'

He rang back in minutes. I don't know if it came from the confidential directories to which the police have access or the Belston Police Club membership list, but it didn't matter.

I punched out the number, praying that no one had won the sweep on Reynolds since we talked to him.

His daughter-in-law answered. She remembered me and agreed to take her cordless phone down the garden to Reynolds. I drummed my fingers while I listened to her footsteps leaving the house and crossing the patio. Voices in the background, then the sergeant's tones in my ear: 'Mr Tyroll, what can I do for you?'

A few questions from me and he told me, all of it except the name of the perpetrator. I thanked him warmly and put the phone down. Alasdair and Sheila were staring at me.

'It wasn't forgeries,' I said. 'It was far, far bigger than that. Renton Street School was wrecked in the big raids on the Midlands, but half of it was still standing. Your grandfather, at the Town Hall, needed somewhere to store unissued ration books and he used the standing part of the school. Like he said in his letter – there was a fire-watch team on the building every night, he thought it was secure, but one night in 1943, someone laid out the fire-watchers and stole a quarter of a million new ration books!'

The audience gaped. 'A quarter of a million!' Sheila exclaimed. 'But Mrs Cassidy said they fetched eight to ten quid on the black market! That's up to two million quid – in the forties – that's, that's God knows how much now – billions probably!'

I nodded. 'They wouldn't have sold them piecemeal, they'd have had to shift them in bulk, but if they only got a pound each, they still netted a huge fortune. What's more, they got clean away.'

'Why?' said Alasdair. 'What did the letter mean about that?'

'The government wouldn't let the police do anything about it because they didn't want to shake public faith in the rationing system. So they let two hundred and fifty thousand bent books go out and the blokes who did it walked away with the loot. No wonder your grandfather was sick about it, Sheila. It was everything he hated. Dishonesty, a blow at the war effort, a cover-up by the government, and he got blamed by those who knew and the guys who did it got away!'

'And who did it?' she said. 'Who lived on to set the dogs on Grandpa and Cassidy and us?'

'If he's right about the photo, it can only be one of three people.'

'Is he right about the photo?' Alasdair asked, playing Devil's Advocate.

'He is,' I said. 'Pete thought it wasn't a Victory party, and noted that the clock said five to four. He thought it was illegal afternoon boozing, but I'll bet that's four in the morning. They've just finished the job and they're celebrating!'

'Can't prove it isn't VE Day or VJ Day,' said Alasdair, and for a moment I thought I couldn't. Then I raked among Pete's papers and found it. The blackboard transcription.

I showed it to him. 'It's not a darts fixture,' I said. 'It's a football match. Look!' I rewrote it:

L.B. LEAGUE

THIS SUNDAY

EAGLE & PUMP
v
THE BULL

2.30

'Plausible,' agreed Alasdair, 'but it might still be a darts match.'

'Oh no, it isn't. L.B. was Lady Belston who sponsored the pub football teams league. The Eagle and Pump was the pub where the picture was taken and the Bull had the best team in the league. Ask Sergeant Reynolds, if you can stand listening to his sporting reminiscences.'

'Could still be 1945,' he said.

'No, it couldn't,' I said, 'because the Bull was bombed, around the time of the V2 rockets in 1944. I don't think there were V2s around here, but that's when Reynolds says it happened and the league broke up. They never played again because four of the Bull's players were killed. That picture was taken about four in the morning in 1943!'

He flung up both hands. 'I concede, governor.'

'Then whoever set it up, whoever is still covering it, is in that picture?' said Sheila.

'That's right,' I said. 'That's what your grandfather thought and he must be right.'

'But who is it?' said Alasdair.

'It has to have been Watson or Thompson or Berry,' I said. 'The rest are dead. Where are Pete's pictures of those three?'

28

Total confusion reigned. Alasdair and I went backwards and forwards over Pete's prints, straining to find anything recognisable in his gallery of old men.

Sheila walked out, impatiently, but came back later with a tray of coffee.

'You see!' she said, as she deposited the tray on top of the gallery of aged faces. 'You can't get at it that way. That'd only work if you knew him, if you'd ever seen him. So far as we know, you haven't. It'll never work!'

She was right and we knew it. We had narrowed it down to one of those three and now we couldn't get anywhere. We weren't even sure that all of them were still alive, we didn't know where they were or what they had become or what they called themselves. It was the last and most important question. Unless we could answer it the mad, deadly game would go on.

We drank coffee and stared despondently at the pictures. None of us had an idea.

Jayne buzzed on the intercom to tell me John Parry was in the waiting-room. 'Send him in!' I said, thinking that he might as well come and share our dead end.

Acting Detective Inspector Parry has two basic expressions, a straight deadpan and a wide, self-satisfied grin. I wasn't best pleased to see that he was wearing the latter.

'Well, lady and gentleman,' he announced, 'the news gets better. Gibson has coughed it all. He's charged with two murders which my bosses are prepared to prosecute now Naylor's dead and Whitehall says it was an unofficial job anyway.'

'Great,' I said, without enthusiasm. 'I bet he didn't tell you who he was working for, did he?'

'Well, of course not. He doesn't know, does he? He's done black bag jobs for Naylor for a good few years, but Naylor was never daft enough to tell him what they were about.'

'Then we're still stymied,' I said.

'But I thought you'd got a good lead through old Reggie Reynolds?' he said. 'That's why I've come. So you brilliant amateur sleuths can tell a poor plod who to arrest.'

'So I had. Thanks to Sergeant Reynolds we know exactly what it was about,' and I told him.

'*Ach y fi!*' he exclaimed. 'A quarter of a million wartime quids! Or half a million or maybe more! Whoever set that up, if he's still alive, he must own the whole bloody country by now!'

'He's still alive,' I said, 'because if he wasn't nobody would have set Naylor and Gibson on to Walter Brown and Cassidy

183

and Sheila and me. And until we can prove who it is we're still targets.'

'Damn!' he said, and shook his big head. 'And you haven't any idea?'

I shoved the heap of pictures across at him. 'Not unless you recognise someone among those. But then, maybe he doesn't look like any of them. Perhaps he's had a face-lift and dyes his hair and looks thirty.'

The room fell silent again while John shuffled through the pictures, Alasdair rolled a cigarette and Sheila stared out of the window. I just went on drinking coffee.

'That one's a bit like someone,' remarked Parry, after several runs through the prints. 'Don't you think?'

He picked out a picture and laid it in front of me. It was a plump, round-faced man, with thick silver hair.

'They're all a bit like someone,' I said, but I studied the picture. Somewhere at the back of my mind a faint bell rang, but I refused to be carried away.

'What do you think, Alasdair?' I turned the picture towards him and he leaned back, squinting at it through his cigarette smoke. 'Could be,' he said, after studying it, 'could be.'

He went on squinting at it, then suddenly leaned forward and swivelled my computer monitor towards him. 'Give us your keyboard, governor!' he demanded.

Bewildered I pushed the keyboard across the desk. He tapped in a few rapid letters and figures and sprang out of his chair. 'Don't touch that!' he said, and disappeared out of the door.

The three of us looked at each other and the open door and shrugged helplessly. Alasdair's feet could be heard, pounding up the stairs. I hoped that my quirky assistant had had a genuine inspiration of some kind.

In three minutes he tumbled back downstairs and into my office, dropped back into his chair and punched more keys on the computer. A smile crossed his face and he swung the monitor back towards me.

'What about him?' he asked.

Most of the screen was filled by a black and white photograph. It was, indeed, a plump, prosperous-looking individual with thick, expensively cut silver hair. I stared and my tongue fumbled for a name. I had seen that face – in the local press and in the national press.

'It might be,' I said. 'It might well be.' The longer I looked the more I saw the resemblance, but I was terribly afraid of misleading myself. 'Who is he?'

'Don't you know?' said Alasdair and touched the keyboard again. The photograph vanished upwards, to be replaced by a screen full of text.

'What's this?' I asked.

'A biography from a computer Encyclopaedia of Biography. It's on my machine upstairs.'

I read while my mind was full of the thudding sound of things falling into place. Now I knew how that unholy alliance between Naylor and Kerrenwood's Security was formed, and why a fifty-year-old crime was still important, and why it had been a serious mistake to give my name to Kerrenwood's Personnel office and ask about Berry. That had only convinced them I knew more than I did. The words in front of me even explained why there wasn't a Berry on the pensions list at Kerrenwood's.

'Lord Muckamuck!' I exclaimed as I reached the end.

'Who?' they all asked.

'It was little Mrs Cassidy's nickname for him,' I explained, and I read the screen aloud. '"Lord Kerrenwood, born Anthony Norman Berry, 15th August 1920 at Belston, then in Staffordshire. After a number of employments as a young man he entered the chemical dyes business in 1948, purchasing an interest in a small company at Kerren Wood, Staffordshire. In the 1950s he became sole proprietor of the company and turned its output to plastics. The success of this change allowed him to open branches of Kerrenwood Enterprises in many parts of Britain. Further diversification into waste management in the 1960s made the company hugely profitable. The organisation has always remained privately owned under Lord Kerrenwood's chairmanship. Although ennobled in 1980, and despite his friendships with prominent politicians, Lord Kerrenwood has never sought a political career, though he is known to have been an adviser on industrial, labour and financial matters to more than one Prime Minister. In recent years his company has attracted criticism through its large political donations and its controversial waste reclamation policies."'

They were still staring. 'Lord Muckamuck!' I repeated. 'Cassidy worked for him for years, his security thugs backed up Naylor, he advised Prime Ministers and bunged their party, and all out of the Renton Street ration book robbery! Now you know who to arrest, Inspector Parry.'

The big Welshman shook his head slowly. 'Too late,' he said. 'Too bloody late, boyo.'

'What do you mean?' asked Sheila.

'It was on the news this morning,' he said. 'Kerrenwood died late last night – of a stroke. They said he was in bed, holding the telephone. Trying to summon medical assistance, they said.' He shook his head again. 'He wasn't calling for any doctor. He'd just heard from his pals in Whitehall that you'd lumbered Naylor and Gibson.'

He turned to Sheila. 'You got them all, Sheila. Game, set and match to Australia.'

And that was it. After those frenzied days we were sitting round my littered desk, each trying to adjust to this sudden stop.

I couldn't prevent my mind from asking more questions, though I knew they would never be answered now. What about the deaths among that little bunch of bandits in the back bar of the Eagle and Pump? Were they really unconnected or was there some kind of squabbling over the spoils afterwards? Did that car go into a canal by accident or had its driver threatened Kerrenwood? Was it really an angry husband or boyfriend who got away with stabbing Alan Thorpe? Did Watson and Thompson move away? Were they peacefully dead or in comfortable retirement somewhere? Or down one of Kerrenwood's chemical pits? Did Howard know who and what he was protecting? Or Saffary? Who put Naylor on the case? No answers.

'Put the picture up again,' I told Alasdair, and with a few deft keystrokes he did so.

I sipped the last of my cold coffee while I sat and stared again at the photograph. It was hard to see in this plump, sleek baron any trace of the sharp-featured young man in the pub photograph, the devious young man 'who always thought he was smarter than everyone else'. But so he had been – almost. He had merely reckoned without a Town Hall clerk with a different belief – a belief in doing what was right – and all his ill-gotten gains hadn't saved him in the end from a lonely frightened death.

For more than fifty years he had used his loot to climb and grab, to make more money and to buy what only money can buy – power. And all the time he must have been afraid of the telephone call that had come last night, to tell him he was on the brink of being exposed.

'Lord Muckamuck,' I murmured again, and switched the screen off.

We celebrated that night with the best meal the Jubilee Room could provide, Sheila and I, Alasdair, Claude, John Parry and Dr Mac, and I gave the last toast – to an honest, upright, fearless public servant called Walter Brown, who I had come to respect and who I think I would have liked if I'd got to know him better.

Once the formalities were over, Sheila was able to arrange her grandfather's cremation. Where she scattered his ashes she wouldn't say. 'It was his favourite place,' she said. 'I'll take you there one day, but not now.'

'One day' – there weren't many days left before her leave ran out. Far too soon we were at Heathrow, making awkward goodbyes. At the boarding gate she took something from her handbag and pinned it into my tie. It was an opal pin with a boomerang on it.

'I can't take that,' I protested. 'It was your grandfather's.'

She shook her head. 'I gave it to him because I loved him,' she said. 'He's gone and I love you, Christopher Tyroll. Besides, I know it's your birthstone too and it'll remind you about the boomerang in me. I'll be back.'

In minutes I was watching the big jet lift and vanish into the clouds.

By late afternoon I was back at my desk. Darren Gormley's committal was due in a couple of days and I needed to prepare for it. I had no intention of letting Saffary out of the Traffic Cone Stores.